My Father's Last Letter

Ruskin Bond is known for his signature simplistic and witty writing style. He is the author of several bestselling short stories, novellas, collections, essays and children's books; and has contributed a number of poems and articles to various magazines and anthologies. At the age of twenty-three, he won the prestigious John Llewellyn Rhys Prize for his first novel, *The Room on the Roof*. He was also the recipient of the Padma Shri in 1999, Lifetime Achievement Award by the Delhi Government in 2012 and the Padma Bhushan in 2014.

Born in 1934, Ruskin Bond grew up in Jamnagar, Shimla, New Delhi and Dehradun. Apart from three years in the UK, he has spent all his life in India, and now lives in Landour, Mussoorie, with his adopted family.

RUSKIN BOND

My Father's Last Letter

RUPA

Published by
Rupa Publications India Pvt. Ltd 2023
7/16, Ansari Road, Daryaganj
New Delhi 110002

Sales centres:
Bengaluru Chennai
Hyderabad Jaipur Kathmandu
Kolkata Mumbai Prayagraj

Copyright © Ruskin Bond 2023

This is a work of fiction. Names, characters, places and incidents are either the product of the author's imagination or are used fictitiously and any resemblance to any actual person, living or dead, events or locales is entirely coincidental.

All rights reserved.
No part of this publication may be reproduced, transmitted, or stored in a retrieval system, in any form or by any means, electronic, mechanical, photocopying, recording or otherwise, without the prior permission of the publisher.

P-ISBN: 978-93-5702-315-3
E-ISBN: 978-93-5702-318-4

Second impression 2023

10 9 8 7 6 5 4 3 2

Printed in India

This book is sold subject to the condition that it shall not, by way of trade or otherwise, be lent, resold, hired out, or otherwise circulated, without the publisher's prior consent, in any form of binding or cover other than that in which it is published.

CONTENTS

Introduction — vii

1. My Father's Last Letter — 1
2. Letter to My Father — 8
3. Life with Father — 12
4. Mother and Stepfather — 27
5. Grandpa Fights an Ostrich — 35
6. Grandfather's Earthquake — 39
7. A Tiger in the House — 44
8. The Old Gramophone — 49
9. The Garden of Memories — 52
10. Life with Uncle Ken — 59
11. At Sea with Uncle Ken — 82
12. Uncle Ken's Feathered Foes — 89
13. Escape from Java — 94
14. A Week in the Jungle — 115

INTRODUCTION

I wonder what the slivers that make up our relationships with our fathers look like: Do we want to become like them? Do we judge ourselves for not measuring up to their standards? Do they make the world feel safe and secure? In one's lifetime, there are very few people whose absence leaves as deep an imprint as their presence does. A father is one such person in his child's life. My father was not only my guide and teacher—who helped me navigate life at home, in foreign lands and at sea—but also my closest friend and confidante. He was the one constant in my life, even as the world around me kept changing.

My Father's Last Letter is an ode to the man who shaped me in countless ways. 'Life with Father' perhaps comes closest to capturing the deep bond I shared with my father, and how he inspired my love for reading, classical music and exploring the world. In 'Escape from Java', I relive an adventurous journey my father and I undertook. I did not know it then, but those early years I spent with him were the most blissful and carefree days of my life. I have also included stories about two other men who played a significant role in my life—my grandfather and my uncle. Through anecdotal tales, like 'Grandpa Fights an Ostrich', 'A Tiger in the House' and 'Uncle Ken's Feathered Foes', I have tried to capture their eccentric natures and effervescent personalities that often landed us in trouble.

I hope this book brings back your warm memories of your loved ones, dear reader, and reminds you to not take them for granted. Hold onto your father's hand as you embark on the journey of life and build your own special catalogue of memories!

Ruskin Bond

MY FATHER'S LAST LETTER

1944. The war dragged on. No sooner was I back in prep school than my father was transferred to Calcutta. In some ways this was a good thing because my sister Ellen was there, living with 'Calcutta Granny,' and my father could live in his own home for a change. Granny had been living on Park Lane ever since Grandfather had died.

It meant, of course, that my father couldn't come to see me in Simla during my mid-term holidays. But he wrote regularly—once a week, on an average. The War was coming to an end, peace was in the air, but there was also talk of the British leaving India as soon as the war was over. In his letters my father spoke of the preparations he was making towards that end. Obviously he saw no future for us in a free India. He was not an advocate of the Empire but he took a pragmatic approach to the problems of the day. There would be a new school for me in England, he said, and meanwhile he was selling off large segments of his stamp collection so that we'd have some money to start life afresh when he left the Royal Air Force (RAF). There was also his old mother to look after, and my sister Ellen and a baby brother, William, who was to be caught in no-man's land.

I did not concern myself too much with the future. Scout camps at Tara Devi and picnics at the Brockhurst tennis courts were diversions in a round of classes, games, dormitory inspections and evening homework. We could shower in the evenings, a welcome change from the tubs of my former school; and we did not have to cover our nudity—there were no nuns in attendance, only our prefects, who were there to see that we didn't scream the place down.

Did we have sexual adventures? Of course we did. It would have been unreasonable to expect a horde of eight to twelve-year-olds to take no interest in those parts of their anatomy which were undergoing constant change during puberty. But it did not go any further than a little clandestine masturbation in the dormitories late at night. There were no scandals, no passionate affairs, at least none that I can recall. We were at the age of inquisitive and innocent enquiry; not (as yet) the age of emotional attachment or experimentation.

Sex was far down our list of priorities; far behind the exploits of the new comic-book heroes—Captain Marvel, Superman, the Green Lantern and others of their ilk. They had come into the country in the wake of the American troops, and looked like they would stay after everyone had gone. We modelled ourselves on our favourite heroes, giving each other names like Bulletman or Wonderman.

Our exploits, however, did not go far beyond the spectacular pillow-fights that erupted every now and then between the lower and upper dormitories, or one section of a dormitory and another. Those fluffy feather pillows, lovingly stitched together by fond mothers (or the darzi sitting on the verandah), would sometimes come apart, resulting in a storm of feathers sweeping across the dorm. On one occasion, the headmaster's wife, alerted by all the noise, rushed into the dorm, only to be greeted by a feather pillow full in the bosom. Mrs Priestley was a large-bosomed woman—we called her breasts 'nutcrackers'—and the pillow burst against them. She slid to the ground, buried in down. As punishment we all received the flat of her hairbrush on our posteriors. Canings were given only in the senior school.

Mrs Priestley played the piano, her husband the violin. They practised together in the assembly hall every evening. They had no children and were not particularly fond of children, as far as I could tell. In fact, Mrs Priestley had a positive antipathy for certain boys and lost no opportunity in using her brush on them. Mr Priestley showed a marked preference for upper-class English boys, of whom there were a few. He was lower middle-class himself (as I discovered later).

Some good friends and companions during my two-and-a-half prep school years were Peter Blake, who did his hair in a puff like Alan Ladd; Brian Abbott, a quiet boy who boasted only of his father's hunting exploits—Abbott was a precursor to Jim Corbett, but never wrote anything; Riaz Khan, a good-natured, fun-loving boy; and Bimal Mirchandani, who grew up to become a Bombay industrialist. I don't know what happened to the others.

As I have said, I kept my father's letters, but the only one that I was able to retain (apart from some of the postcards) was the last one, which I reproduce here.

It is a good example of the sort of letters he wrote to me, and you can see why I hung on to it.

AA Bond 108485 (RAF)
c/o 231 Group
Rafpost
Calcutta 20/8/44

My dear Ruskin,

Thank you very much for your letter received a few days ago. I was pleased to hear that you were quite well and learning hard. We are all quite O.K. here, but I am still not strong enough to go to work after the recent attack of malaria I had. I was in hospital for a long time and that is the reason why you did not get a letter from me for several weeks.

I have now to wear glasses for reading, but I do not use them for ordinary wear—but only when I read or do book work. Ellen does not wear glasses at all now.

Do you need any new warm clothes? Your warm suits must be getting too small. I am glad to hear the rains are practically over in the hills where you are. It will be nice to have sunny days in September when your holidays are on. Do the holidays begin from the 9th of Sept? What will you do? Is there to be a Scouts, Camp at Tara Devi? Or will you catch butterflies on sunny days on the school Cricket Ground? I am glad to hear you have lots of friends. Next year you will be in the top class of the Prep School. You only have 3 months more for the Xmas holidays to come round, when you will be glad to come home, I am sure, to do more Stamp work and Library Study. The New Market is full of book shops here. Ellen loves the market.

I wanted to write before about your writing Ruskin, but forgot. Sometimes I get letters from you written in very small handwriting, as if you wanted to squeeze a lot of news into one sheet of letter paper. It is not good for you or for your eyes, to get into the habit of writing small. I know your handwriting is good and that you came 1st in class for handwriting, but try and form a larger style of writing and do not worry if you can't get all your news into one sheet of paper—but stick to big letters.

We have had a very wet month just passed. It is still cloudy, at night we have to use fans, but during the cold weather it is nice—not too cold like Delhi and not too warm either—but just moderate. Granny is quite well. She and Ellen send you their fond love. The last I heard a week ago, that William and all at Dehra were well also.

We have been without a cook for the past few days. I hope we find a good one before long. There are not many. I wish I could get our Delhi cook, the old man now famous for his 'Black Puddings' which Ellen hasn't seen since we arrived in Calcutta 4 months ago.

I have still got the Records and Gramophone and most of the best books, but as they are all getting old and some not suited to you which are only for children under 8 yrs old—I will give some to William and Ellen and you can pencil now and draws some wonderful animals like camels, elephants, dragons with many heads—cobras—rain clouds shedding buckets of water—tigers with long grass around them—horses with manes and wolves and foxes with bushy hair. Sometimes you can't see much of the animals because there is too much grass covering them or two much hair on the foxes and wolves and too much mane on the horses' necks—or too much rain from the clouds. All this decoration is made up by a sort of heavy scribbling of lines, but through it all one can see some very good shapes of animals, elephants and ostriches and other things. I will send you some.

Well, Ruskin, I hope this finds you well. With fond love from us all. Write again soon, Ever your loving daddy...

◆

It was about two weeks after receiving this letter that I was given the news of my father's death. Those frequent bouts of malaria had undermined his health, and a severe attack of jaundice did the rest. A kind but inept teacher, Mr Murtough, was given the unenviable task of breaking the news to me. He mumbled something about God needing my father more than I did, and of course I knew what had happened and broke down and had to be taken to the infirmary, where I remained for a couple of days. It never made any sense to me why God should have needed my father more than I did, unless of course He envied my father's stamp collection. If God was Love, why did He have to break up the only loving relationship I'd known so far? What would happen to me now, I wondered... Would I live with Calcutta Granny or some other relative or be put away in an orphanage?

Mr Priestley saw me in his office and said I'd be going to my mother when school closed. He said he'd been told that I had kept my father's letters and that if I wished to put them in his safe keeping he'd see that they were not lost. I handed them over—all except the one I've reproduced here.

The day before we broke up for the school holidays, I went to Mr Priestley and asked for my letters. 'What letters?' He looked bemused and irritated. He'd had a trying day. 'My father's letters,' I told him. 'You said you'd keep them for me.' 'Did I? Don't remember. Why should I want to keep your father's letters?' 'I don't know, sir. You put them in your drawer' He opened the drawer, shut it. 'None of your letters here. I'm very busy now, Bond. If I find any of your letters, I'll give them to you.' I was dismissed from his presence.

I never saw those letters again. And I'm glad to say I did not see Mr Priestley again. All he'd given me was a lifelong aversion to violin players.

LETTER TO MY FATHER

My Dear Dad,

Last week I decided to walk from the Dilaram Bazaar to Rajpur, a walk I hadn't undertaken for many years. It's only about five miles, along straight tree-lined road, houses most of the way, but here and there are open spaces where there are fields and patches of sal forest. The road hasn't changed much, but there is far more traffic than there used to be, which makes it noisy and dusty, detracting from the sylvan surroundings. All the same I enjoyed the walk—enjoyed the cool breeze that came down from the hills, the rich variety of trees, the splashes of colour where bougainvillea trailed over porches and enjoyed the passing cyclists and bullock carts, for they were reminders of the old days when cars, trucks and buses were the exception rather than the rule.

A little way above the Dilaram Bazaar, just where the canal goes under the road, stands the old house we used to know as Melville Hall, where three generations of Melvilles had lived. It is now a government office and looks dirty and neglected. Beside it still stands the little cottage, or guest house, where you stayed for a few weeks while the separation from my mother was being made legal. Then I went to live with you in Delhi.

At the time you were a guest of the Melvilles, I was in boarding school, so I did not share the cottage with you, although I was to share a number of rooms, tents and RAF hutments with you during the next two or three years. But of course I knew the Melvilles; I would visit them during school holidays in the years after you died, and they always spoke affectionately of you. One of the sisters was particularly kind to me; I think it was she who gave you the use of the cottage. This was Mrs Chill—she'd lost her husband to cholera during their honeymoon, and never married again. But I always found her cheerful and good-natured, loading me with presents on birthdays and at Christmas. The kindest people are often those who have gone through testing personal tragedies.

A young man on a bicycle stops beside me and asks if I remember him. 'Not with that terrible moustache,' I confess. 'Romi from Sisters Bazaar.' Yes, of course. And I do remember him, although it must be about ten years since we last met; he was just a schoolboy then. Now, he tells me, he's a teacher. Not very well paid, as he works in a small private school. But better than being unemployed, he says. I have to agree.

'You're a good teacher, I'm sure, Romi. And it's still a noble profession...'

He looks pleased as he cycles away. When I see boys on bicycles I am always taken back to my boyhood days in Dehra. The roads in those uncrowded days were ideal for cyclists. Somi on his bicycle, riding down this very road in the light spring rain, provided me with the opening scene for my very first novel, *Room on the Roof,* written a couple of years after I'd said goodbye to Somi and Dehra and even, for a time, India.

That's how I remember him best—on his bicycle, wearing shorts, turban slightly askew, always a song on his lips. He was just fifteen. I was a couple of years older, but wasn't much of a bicycle rider, always falling off the machine when I was supposed to dismount gracefully. On one occasion I went sailing into a buffalo cart and fractured my forearm. Last year when Dr Murti, a senior citizen of the Doon, met me at a local function, he recalled how he had set my arm forty years ago. He was so nice to me that I forbore from telling him that my arm was still crooked.

Strictly an earth man, I have never really felt at ease with my feet off the ground. That's why I've been a walking person for most of my life. In planes, on ships, even in lifts, panic sets in.

As it did on that occasion when I was four or five, and you, Dad, decided to give me a treat by taking me on an Arab dhow across the Gulf of Kutch. Five minutes on that swinging, swaying sailing ship, was enough for me; I became so hysterical that I had to be taken off and rowed back to port. Not that the rowing boat was much better.

And then my mother thought I should go up with her in one those four-winged aeroplanes, a Tiger Moth I think—there's a photograph of it somewhere among my mementos—one of those contraptions that fell out of the sky without much assistance during the first World War. I think you could make them at home. Anyway, in this too I kicked and screamed with such abandon that the poor pilot had to be content with taxiing around the airfield and dropping me off at the first opportunity. That same plane with the same pilot crashed a couple of months later, only reinforcing my fears about machines that could not stay anchored to the ground.

To return to Somi, he was one of those friends I never saw again as an adult, so he remains transfixed in my memory as eternal youth, bright and forever loving... Meeting boyhood friends again after long intervals can often be disappointing, even disconcerting. Mere survival leaves its mark. Success is even more disfiguring. Those who climb to the top of a profession, or who seek the pinnacles of power, usually have to pay a heavy price for it, both physically and spiritually. It sounds like a cliche but it's true that money can't buy good health or a serene state of mind—especially the latter. You can fly to the ends of the earth in search of the best climate or the best medical treatment and the chances are that you will have to keep flying! Poverty is not ennobling—far from it—but it does at least teach you to make the most out of every rule.

I have often dreamt of Somi, and it is always the same dream, year after year, for over forty years. We meet in a fairground, set up on Dehra's old parade-ground which has seen better days. In the dream I am a man but he is still a boy. We wander through the fairground, enjoying all that it has to offer, and when the dream ends we are still in that fairground which probably represents heaven.

Heaven. Is that the real heaven—the perfect place with the perfect companion? And if you and I meet again, Dad, will you look the same, and will I be a small boy or an old man?

In my dreams of you I meet you on a busy street, after many lost years, and you receive me with the same old warmth, but where were you all those missing years? A traveller in another dimension, perhaps, returning occasionally just to see if I am all right.

LIFE WITH FATHER

During my childhood and early boyhood with my father, we were never in one house or dwelling for very long. I think the 'Tennis Bungalow' in Jamnagar (in the grounds of the Ram Vilas Palace) housed us for a couple of years, and that was probably the longest period.

In Jamnagar itself we had at least three abodes—a rambling, leaking old colonial mansion called 'Cambridge House'; a wing of an old palace, the Lal Bagh I think it was called, which was also inhabited by bats and cobras; and the aforementioned 'Tennis Bungalow,' a converted sports pavilion which was really quite bright and airy.

I think my father rather enjoyed changing houses, setting up home in completely different surroundings. He loved rearranging rooms too, so that this month's sitting room became next month's bedroom, and so on; furniture would also be moved around quite frequently, somewhat to my mother's irritation, for she liked having things in their familiar places. She had grown up in one abode (her father's Dehra house) whereas my father hadn't remained anywhere for very long. Sometimes he spoke of making a home in Scotland, beside Loch Lomond, but it was only a distant dream.

The only real stability was represented by his stamp collection, and this he carried around in a large tin trunk, for it was an extensive and valuable collection—there was an album for each country he specialized in: Greece, Newfoundland, British possessions in the Pacific, Borneo, Zanzibar, Sierra Leone; these were some of the lands whose stamps he favoured most...

I did share some of his enthusiasm for stamps, and they gave me a strong foundation in geography and political history, for he went to the trouble of telling me something about the places and people depicted on them—that Pitcairn Island was inhabited largely by mutineers from *H.M.S. Bounty;* that the Solomon Islands were famous for their butterflies; that Britannia still ruled the waves (but only just); that Iraq had a handsome young boy king; that in Zanzibar the Sultan wore a fez; that zebras were exclusive to Kenya, Uganda and Tanganyika; that in America presidents were always changing; and that the handsome young hero on Greek stamps was a Greek god with a sore heel. All this and more, I remember from my stamp-sorting sessions with my father. However, it did not form a bond between him and my mother. She was bored with the whole thing.

◆

My earliest memories don't come in any particular order, but most of them pertain to Jamnagar, where we lived until I was five or six years old.

There was the beach at Balachadi, and I remember picking up seashells and wanting to collect them much as my father collected stamps. When the tide was out I went paddling with some of the children from the palace.

My father set up a schoolroom for the palace children. It was on the ground floor of a rambling old palace, which had a tower and a room on the top. Sometimes I attended my father's classes more as an observer than a scholar. One day I set off on my own to explore the deserted palace, and ascended some wandering steps to the top, where I found myself in a little room full of tiny stained-glass windows. I took turns at each window pane, looking out at a green or red or yellow world. It was a magical room.

Many years later—almost forty years later, in fact—I wrote a story with this room as its setting. It was called 'The Room of Many Colours'* and it had in it a mad princess, a gardener and a snake.

◆

Not all memories are dream-like and idyllic. I witnessed my parents' quarrels from an early age, and later when they resulted in my mother taking off for unknown destinations (unknown to me). I would feel helpless and insecure. My father's hand was always there, and I held it firmly until it was wrenched away by the angel of death.

That early feeling of insecurity was never to leave me, and in adult life, when I witnessed quarrels between people who were close to me, I was always deeply disturbed—more for the children, whose lives were bound to be affected by such emotional discord. But can it be helped? People who marry young, even those who are in love in *Time Stops at Shamli and Other Stories*, do not really know each other. The body chemistry may be right but the harmony of two minds is what makes relationships endure.

Words of wisdom from a disappointed bachelor!

I don't suppose I would have written so much about childhood or even about other children if my own childhood had been all happiness and light. I find that those who have

---

*In *Time Stops at Shamli and Other Stories*.

had contented, normal childhoods, seldom remember much about them; nor do they have much insight into the world of children. Some of us are born sensitive. And, if, on top of that, we are pulled about in different directions (both emotionally and physically), we might just end up becoming writers.

No, we don't become writers in schools of creative writing. We become writers before we learn to write. The rest is simply learning how to put it all together.

♦

I learnt to read from my father but not in his classroom.

The children were older than me. Four of them were princesses, very attractive, but always clad in buttoned-up jackets and trousers. This was a bit confusing for me, because I had at first taken them for boys. One of them used to pinch my cheeks and hug me.

While I thought she was a boy, I rather resented the familiarity. When I discovered she was a girl (I had to be told), I wanted more of it.

I was shy of these boyish princesses, and was to remain shy of girls until I was in my teens.

♦

Between Tennis Bungalow and the palace were lawns and flower beds. One of my earliest memories is of picking my way through a forest of flowering cosmos; to a five-year-old they were almost trees, the flowers nodding down at me in friendly invitation.

Since then, the cosmos has been my favourite flower—fresh, open, uncomplicated—living up to its name, cosmos, the universe as an ordered whole. White, purple and rose, they are at their best in each other's company, growing almost anywhere, in the hills or on the plains, in Europe or tropical America. Waving gently in the softest of breezes, they are both sensuous and beyond sensuality. An early influence!

There were of course rose bushes in the palace grounds, kept tidy and trim and looking very like those in the illustrations in my first copy of *Alice in Wonderland*, a well-thumbed edition from which my father often read to me. (Not the Tenniel illustrations, something a little softer.) I think I have read Alice more often than any other book, with the possible exception of *The Diary of a Nobody*, which I turn to whenever I am feeling a little low. Both books help me to a better appreciation of the absurdities of life.

There were extensive lawns in front of the bungalow, where I could romp around or push my small sister around on a tricycle. She was a backward child, who had been affected by polio and some damage to the brain (having been born prematurely and delivered with the help of forceps), and she was the cross that had to be borne by my parents, together and separately. In spite of her infirmities, Ellen was going to outlive most of us.

◆

Although we lived briefly in other houses, and even for a time in the neighbouring state of Pithadia, Tennis Bungalow was our home for most of the time we were in Jamnagar.

There were several Englishmen working for the Jam Saheb. The port authority was under Commander Bourne, a retired British naval officer. And a large farm (including a turkey farm) was run for the state by a Welsh couple, the Jenkins. I remember the verandah of the Jenkins home, because the side table was always stacked with copies of the humorous weekly, *Punch*, really taken me seriously when I'd said I hated the place.

Oddly enough, we did not stop in Dehra Dun at my grandmother's place. Instead my mother took me straight to the railway station and put me on the night train to Delhi. I don't remember if anyone accompanied me—I must have been too young to travel alone—but I remember being met at the Delhi station by my father in full uniform. It was early summer, and he was in khakis, but the blue RAF cap took my fancy. Come winter, he'd be wearing a dark blue uniform with a different kind of cap, and by then he'd be a flying officer and getting saluted by juniors. Being wartime, everyone was saluting madly, and I soon developed the habit, saluting everyone in sight.

An uncle on my mother's side, Fred Clark, was then the station superintendent at Delhi railway station, and he took us home for breakfast to his bungalow, not far from the station. From the conversation that took place during the meal I gathered that my parents had separated, that my mother was remaining in Dehra Dun, and that henceforth I would be in my father's custody. My sister Ellen was to stay with 'Calcutta Granny'—my father's seventy-year-old mother. The arrangement pleased me, I must admit.

◆

The two years I spent with my father were probably the happiest of my childhood—although, for him, they must have been a period of trial and tribulation. Frequent bouts of malaria had undermined his constitution; the separation from my mother weighed heavily on him, and it could not be reversed; and at the age of eight I was self-willed and demanding.

He did his best for me, dear man. He gave me his time, his companionship, his complete attention.

A year was to pass before I was re-admitted to a boarding school, and I would have been quite happy never to have gone to school again. My year in the convent had been sufficient punishment for uncommitted sins. I felt that I had earned a year's holiday.

It was a glorious year, during which we changed our residence at least four times—from a tent on a flat treeless plain outside Delhi, to a hutment near Humayun's tomb: to a couple of rooms on Atul Grove Road; to a small flat on Hailey Road; and finally to an apartment in Scindia House, facing the Connaught Circus.

We were not very long in the tent and hutment—but long enough for me to remember the scorching winds of June, and the bhisti's hourly visit to douse the khas-khas matting with water. This turned a hot breeze into a refreshing, fragrant zephyr—for about half an hour. And then the dust and the prickly heat took over again. A small table fan was the only luxury.

Except for Sundays, I was alone during most of the day; my father's office in Air Headquarters was somewhere near India Gate. He'd return at about six, tired but happy to find me in good spirits. For although I had no friends during that period, I found plenty to keep me occupied—books, stamps, the old gramophone, hundreds of postcards which he'd collected during his years in England, a scrapbook, albums of photographs... And sometimes I'd explore the jungle behind the tents; but I did not go very far, because of the snakes that proliferated there.

I would have my lunch with a family living in a neighbouring tent, but at night my father and I would eat together. I forget who did the cooking. But he made the breakfast, getting up early to whip up some fresh butter (he loved doing this) and then laying the table with cornflakes or grapenuts, and eggs poached or fried.

The gramophone was a great companion when my father was away. He had kept all the records he had collected in Jamnagar, and these were added to from time to time. There were operatic arias and duets from La Bohéme and Madame Butterfly; ballads and traditional airs rendered by Paul Robeson, Peter Dawson, Richard Crooks, Webster Booth, Nelson Eddy and other tenors and baritones, and of course the great Russian bass, Chaliapin. And there were lighter, music-hall songs and comic relief provided by Gracie Fields (the 'Lancashire Lass'), George Formby with his ukelele, Arthur Askey ('big-hearted' Arthur—he was a tiny chap,) Flanagan and Allen, and a host of other recording artistes. You couldn't just put on some music and lie back and enjoy it. That was the day of the wind-up gramophone, and it had to be wound up fairly vigorously before a 75 rmp record could be played. I enjoyed this chore. The needle, too, had to be changed after almost every record, if you wanted to keep them in decent condition. And the records had to be packed flat, otherwise, in the heat and humidity they were inclined to assume weird shapes and become unplayable.

It was always a delight to accompany my father to one of the record shops in Connaught Place, and come home with a new record by one of our favourite singers.

After a few torrid months in the tent-house and then in a brick hutment, which was even hotter, my father was permitted to rent rooms of his own on Atul Grove Road, a tree-lined lane not far from Connaught Place, which was then the hub and business centre of New Delhi. Keeping me with him had been quite unofficial; his superiors were always wanting to know why my mother wasn't around to look after me. He was really hoping that the war would end soon, so that he could take me to England and put me in a good school there. He had been selling some of his more valuable stamps and had put quite a bit in the bank.

One evening he came home with a bottle of Scotch whisky. This was most unusual, because I had never seen him drinking—not even beer. Had he suddenly decided to hit the bottle?

The mystery was solved when an American officer dropped in to have dinner with us (having a guest for dinner was a very rare event), and our cook excelled himself by producing succulent pork chops, other viands and vegetables, and my favourite chocolate pudding. Before we sat down to dinner, our guest polished off several pegs of whisky (my father had a drink too), and after dinner they sat down to go through some of my father's stamp albums. The American collector bought several stamps, and we went to bed richer by a couple of thousand rupees.

That it was possible to make money out of one's hobby was something I was to remember when writing became my passion.

When my father had a bad bout of malaria and was admitted to the Military Hospital, I was on my own for about ten days. Our immediate neighbours, an elderly Anglo-Indian couple, kept an eye on me, only complaining that I went through a tin of guava jam in one sitting. This tendency to over-indulge has been with me all my life. Those stringy convent meals must have had something to do with it.

I made one friend during the Atul Grove days. He was a boy called Joseph—from South India, I think—who lived next door. In the evenings we would meet on a strip of grassland across the road and engage in wrestling bouts which were watched by an admiring group of servants' children from a nearby hostelry.

We also had a great deal of fun in the trenches that had been dug along the road in case of possible Japanese air raids (there had been one on Calcutta). During the monsoon they filled with rainwater, much to the delight of the local children, who used them as miniature swimming pools. They were then quite impracticable as air raid shelters.

Of course, the real war was being fought in Burma and the Far East, but Delhi was full of men in uniform. When winter came, my father's khakis were changed for dark blue RAF caps and uniforms, which suited him nicely. He was a good-looking man, always neatly dressed; on the short side but quite sturdy. He was over forty when he had joined up—hence the office job, deciphering (or helping to create) codes and ciphers. He was quite secretive about it all (as indeed he was supposed to be), and as he confided in me on almost every subject but his work, he was obviously a reliable Intelligence officer.

He did not have many friends in Delhi. There was the occasional visit to Uncle Fred near the railway station, and sometimes he'd spend a half-hour with Mr Rankin, who owned a large drapery shop at Connaught Circus, where officers' uniforms were tailored. Mr Rankin was another enthusiastic stamp collector, and the two of them would get together in Mr Rankin's back office and exchange stamps or discuss new issues. I think the drapery establishment closed down after the War. Mr Rankin was always extremely well dressed, as though he had stepped straight out of Saville Row and on to the steamy streets of Delhi.

My father and I explored old tombs and monuments, but going to the pictures was what we did most, if he was back from work fairly early.

Connaught Place was well served with cinemas—the Regal,

Rivoli, Odeon and Plaza, all very new and shiny—and they exhibited the latest Hollywood and British productions. It was in these cinemas that I discovered the beautiful Sonja Henie, making love on skates and even getting married on ice; Nelson and Jeanette making love in duets; Errol Flynn making love on the high seas; and Gary Cooper and Claudette Colbert making love in the bedroom (*Bluebeard's Eighth Wife*). I made careful listings of all the films I saw, including their casts, and to this day I can give you the main performers in almost any film made in the 1940s. And I still think it was cinema's greatest decade, with the stress on good story, clever and economical direction (films seldom exceeded 120-minutes running time), superb black and white photography, and actors and actresses who were also personalities in their own right. The era of sadistic thrills, gore, and psychopathic killers was still far away. The accent was on entertainment—naturally enough, when the worst war in history had spread across Europe, Asia and the Pacific.

◆

When my father broached the subject of sending me to a boarding school, I used every argument I could think of to dissuade him. The convent school was still fresh in my memory and I had no wish to return to any institution remotely resembling it—certainly not after almost a year of untrammelled freedom and my father's companionship.

'Why do you want to send me to school again?' I asked. 'I can learn more at home. I can read books, I can write letters, I can even do sums!'

'Not bad for a boy of nine,' said my father. 'But I can't teach you algebra, physics and chemistry.'

'I don't want to be a chemist.'

'Well, what would you like to be when you grow up?'

'A tap-dancer.'

'We've been seeing too many pictures. Everyone says I spoil you.'

I tried another argument. 'You'll have to live on your own again. You'll feel lonely.'

'That can't be helped, son. But I'll come to see you as often as I can. You see, they're posting me to Karachi for some time, and then I'll be moved again—they won't allow me to keep you with me at some of these places. Would you like to stay with your mother?'

I shook my head.

'With Calcutta Granny?'

'I don't know her.'

'When the War's over I'll take you with me to England.

But for the next year or two we must stay here. I've found a nice school for you.'

'Another convent?'

'No, it's a prep school for boys in Simla. And I may be able to get posted there during the summer.'

'I want to see it first,' I said.

'We'll go up to Simla together. Not now—in April or May, before it gets too hot. It doesn't matter if you join school a bit later—I know you'll soon catch up with the others.'

There was a brief trip to Dehra Dun. I think my father felt that there was still a chance of a reconciliation with my mother. But her affair with the businessman was too far gone. His own wife had been practically abandoned and left to look after the photography shop she'd brought along with her dowry. She was a stout lady with high blood pressure, who once went in search of my mother and stepfather with an axe. Fortunately, they were not at home that day and she had to vent her fury on the furniture.

In later years, when I got to know her quite well, she told me that my father was a very decent man, who treated her with great courtesy and kindness on the one occasion they met.

I remember we stayed in a little hotel or boarding house just off the Eastern Canal Road.

Dehra was a green and leafy place. The houses were separated by hedges, not walls, and the residential areas were criss-crossed by little lanes bordered by hibiscus or oleander shrubs.

We were soon back in Delhi.

My parents' separation was final and it was to be almost two years before I saw my mother again.

MOTHER AND STEPFATHER

When I got down from the train at the Dehra Dun station—one of several boys in the 'Dehra party'—I expected to be met by my mother, or at least someone from her household. But although I waited on the platform for—at least an hour, until it was emptied of passengers, porters and vendors of every description, no one who looked even remotely familiar came up to where I sat on my tin trunk, beside my bedding roll, attaché case and hockey stick. Even the platform dogs had slunk away, for I had nothing to offer them, my school sandwiches having been consumed the night before.

Other children had been met by parents and relatives and had dispersed to their homes. A junior station official came up and asked me if I was waiting for someone.

'I think so,' I said. 'T'll wait a little longer.'

A feeling of insecurity began to creep over me—a feeling that was to recur from time to time and which was to become part of my mental luggage for the rest of my life.

After another half-hour of futile waiting, I got a porter to carry my luggage out to the tonga stand—there were no taxis then—and piling into one of these rickety pony-drawn contraptions, I gave the tongawallah the address of my grandmother's house on the Old Survey Road, and set off in the hope that house and grandmother still existed. It was at least three years since I had seen either.

Granny was there, of course, feeding her black pariah dog, Crazy, who recognized me, leapt on me, licked my face and then, to show his delight, ran three times around the house—a habit of his when pleased! Granny's dog had more character than any pedigreed canine in the neighbourhood.

Granny, a heavy-set, heavy-jowled woman, was a taciturn person who displayed no great joy at seeing me, but she was both surprised and concerned at my unexpected arrival in a tonga.

'Weren't you met at the station?'

'No,' I said.

'Well, they don't live here. Do you know where to go?'

'No.'

'Then I'd better come with you, I suppose.'

With great reluctance she got into the tonga. It was drawn by a white pony, and she was prejudiced against white ponies, believing them to be unruly and ill-natured. But this one got us to Dalanwala and my stepfather's rented house without mishap.

After a good deal of calling out and knocking on doors, a servant appeared and told us that the sahib and memsahib were away on a shikar trip and wouldn't be back till evening. Grandmother asked the cook-cum-bearer to prepare lunch for me and then, dismissing the tonga with the innocent white pony, hailed another that was passing along the road. This one was drawn by a piebald pony. Apparently she did not feel threatened by it, or by the tongawallah, a scruffy-looking chap with yellow teeth, for she got in with some aplomb and rode off to her house, having done her duty by me. I never could fathom my maternal grandmother, or what lay behind her taciturnity. 'Calcutta Granny' I had seen only once. My maternal grandfather had died when I was just a year old. So I'd missed the companionship and attention that grandparents can often give. My father had been the best of companions, but now there was no one to take his place.

My grandmother was a strange person. She sat alone in the evenings, playing Patience, a card game which does not require another player. Her tenant, Miss Kellner, did the same thing, but she was a cripple who could not move from her chair. It never occurred to either of them to play each other at cards, though Miss Kellner did occasionally go out (in a sedan chair) to bridge parties in other European or Anglo-Indian households.

In some of my children's stories I have written about fun-loving grandfathers and doting grandmothers, but this was just wishful thinking on my part. Grandmother could be kind, but she did not *dote* on her grandchildren. If you told her you were hungry, you were presented with a slice of bread and butter. When I was really hungry, I slipped across to Miss Kellner's part of the house. She had a well-stocked larder and would ply me with cakes, scones, meringues, ginger biscuits and other delicacies.

During the school holidays, I would often go to see Miss Kellner (on the pretext of visiting Granny), and she never disappointed me.

My mother and stepfather returned from their shikar trip late at night. Before that, I'd made the acquaintance of the cook, an ayah and a baby half-brother. There was also a small garden to explore, and an orchard of guava trees. I was beginning to find that trees gave me a feeling of security, as well as privacy and a calm haven.

I should say here now that my stepfather, Mr Hari, was in no way cruel or unkind to me. He was, however, something of a playboy, who loved drinking, dancing, hunting, party-going, in other words, *la dolce vita*—and he had little or no time for a boy of ten who had just been dumped on him because there was nowhere else I could go. He did not make any attempt to relate to me and that was just as well, because he hadn't the sensitivity to make a go of being a 'father'. Even with his own children (previous and future) he led by failure rather than by example. He seemed unaware of them most of the time. Only in his later years, particularly after my mother's death, did he begin to take an interest in what we were doing.

'Calcutta Granny' died that winter, and as a result my sister Ellen also arrived, accompanied by a nanny. In her box were some of my books but none of my father's stamps. Had they *all* been sold, I wondered, and if they had, where was the money? No one seemed to know.

The nanny was sent back to Calcutta and replaced by the ayah. The household now consisted of my mother and stepfather (when they were at home), the cook-bearer, the ayah, Ellen, my baby brother William, and my baby half-brother Harold. Mr Hari's children from his first wife lived with their mother behind their shop in the town. His daughter, Premela, was one day to take over the responsibility of looking after my sister, Ellen.

From the start I insisted on having a room of my own, something I was always to insist on, even if it meant sleeping in a tin shed in the garden. My first room wasn't a tin shed; it was a nice room, with a view of the lichi trees and the road and a large open plot on the other side of the road. Dehra was then a place of open spaces and this one beckoned to me. I set out for a stroll—the first of many through the lanes and byways of this leafy little town, and the fields and tea gardens that once surrounded it.

Inevitably, one of my walks took me to my grandmother's house. She was out that day on one of her rare visits to the

Allahabad Bank, so I walked over to Miss Kellner's side of the house and found her sitting in the sun, writing letters. She was a great letter-writer, even though she held the quill pen in an awkward way, her hands being deformed.

She looked at me over her pince-nez and asked me to sit down on a mora beside her. She was unable to stand; her feet and hands were crippled since her early childhood in Calcutta. When she was a baby, a fond uncle had been tossing her in the air and catching her as she came down. Something had happened to distract his attention. He'd tossed her high in the air but out of reach, and she'd landed on the floor with a thud. That had been over sixty years ago. Miss Kellner's parents had died, leaving her a good income, and she had lived on, settling in Dehra Dun because of its gentler climate and restful atmosphere.

As she was unobtrusive and regular with her payments she was the ideal tenant for my grandmother. She liked having visitors, and as I have already mentioned, her larder was well stocked.

On this early visit, she invited me to play 'Snap' with her. This was a simple but rather noisy card game in which the players shouted 'Snap!' whenever they put down cards that matched. I forget the other rules and I never became a card-player, but Miss Kellner and I enjoyed ourselves hugely for half an hour, at the end of which time she plied me with cakes and meringues.

Another elderly person who befriended me was Dhuki, my grandmother's gardener. He was always down on his haunches, weeding the flower beds, and I could talk to him without looking up, as a child must do when talking to an upright adult. I'd ask Dhuki the names of different flowers and of course he knew them all, although he preferred to use the Hindustani 'gulab' for rose and 'genda' for marigold. Otherwise he'd use most of the English names—phlox, zinnia, gerbera, sweet-pea, geranium. Grandmother did not care for the smell of marigolds and tossed them out, but Miss Kellner allowed them to flourish on her side of the house—she said they kept the mosquitoes away!

Dhuki was a skinny, spindle-legged forty-year-old who looked sixty. He and his wife (who was sometimes heard but seldom seen) had been producing a baby a year for quite some time, and there were about twelve survivors ranging in age from six months to sixteen years. They could be seen playing in the guava orchard behind the bungalow and Dhuki did not encourage them to venture into the front garden.

I seemed to get on with old or elderly people, and at this point in my life had no desire to make young friends.

I began to read whatever books came my way. As very few did, I could not be choosy. But whatever they were—cheap thriller or Victorian classic or even erotica (there was some of that around too)—it provided me with an escape from the reality of my situation. And it was during those first winter holidays in Dehra that I became a bookworm and, ultimately, a book lover and writer in embryo.

◆

When my mother and Mr Hari went off on their two or three-day shikar trips, I was usually left at home; but on one or two occasions they took me along, hoping perhaps to instil in me a love for big-game hunting!

I have described one of these jaunts before, in a story, 'Copperfield in the Jungle', so I will just summarize it by saying that my boredom and ennui were relieved by the discovery of a bookshelf in the Forest Rest House where we were staying. And while the great hunters were dashing off into the jungle with their guns (and frequently coming back empty-handed), I discovered several authors who were to give me considerable pleasure then and in the years to come: M.R. James (*Ghost Stories of An Antiquary*), P.G. Wodehouse (*Love among the Chickens* was my introduction to PGW), and A.A. Milne (with *The Red House Mystery*). I was always to prefer Milne's adult stories and plays to his children's stories. (I think he did, too, in the end.) Toy animals voicing human sentiments never did fascinate me. Appealing though animals may be as pets or in the wild, their civilization is different from ours. A better one, possibly; but distinct from ours. The only time I found an animal take an interest in a book was when, quite recently, a monkey got into my Mussoorie home and tore several of my manuscripts to shreds. Some might say that he was only doing what I should have done myself, but even my worst critics haven't gone that far. I like animals but I refuse to be sentimental about them.

Back in the 1940s, even though the visual media was restricted to the cinema, books were scarce commodities in small-town India. Anyone who was hooked on reading had to go in search of books.

Poking around in the back verandah of Granny's house on Old Survey Road, I found a number of books, obviously untouched for years, tucked away in a chest of drawers. I had never seen my grandmother read anything apart from letters, so they could not have been hers. The name 'E. Sims' was inscribed in some of them, and I learnt later that she was probably a great-aunt who had died some years previously.

A few of the books were religious tracts, obviously unsuitable for an enquiring mind, but several Victorian novelists were included in the small collection, and there were two or three novels by Dickens. I picked up *Nicholas Nickleby* and carried it back to my stepfather's rented house in Dalanwala.

A fortnight later I was back in Granny's back verandah, and this time I came up with a book of stories about South Africa, *The Little Karoo* by Pauline Smith, and *The Virginian* by Owen Wister, a novel that was a precursor of the modern 'Western'. Both books had 'E. Sims' on the flyleaf, and it was clear that her tastes were nothing if not eclectic.

I never could find out much about 'E. Sims,' other than that she was a distant relative, but she certainly played a formative role in my development as a reader (and possibly as a writer), because I devoured almost all the books in that small collection (including such diverse works as *Little Women* and *The Invisible Man*) and to this day remain ready to read almost anything provided it has tone, style and substance.

GRANDPA FIGHTS AN OSTRICH

Before my grandfather joined the Indian Railways, he worked for a few years on the East African Railways, and it was during that period that he had his now famous encounter with the ostrich. My childhood was frequently enlivened by this oft-told tale of his, and I give it here in his own words—or as well as I can remember them!

While engaged in the laying of a new railway line, I had a miraculous escape from an awful death. I lived in a small township, but my work lay some twelve miles away, and I had to go to the work site and back on horseback.

One day, my horse had a slight accident, so I decided to do the journey on foot, being a great walker in those days. I also knew of a short cut through the hills that would save me about six miles.

This short cut went through an ostrich farm—or 'camp', as it was called. It was the breeding season. I was fairly familiar with the ways of ostriches, and knew that male birds were very aggressive in the breeding season, ready to attack on the slightest provocation, but I also knew that my dog would scare away any bird that might try to attack me. Strange though it may seem, even the biggest ostrich (and some of them grow to a height of nine feet) will run faster than a racehorse at the sight of even a small dog. So, I felt quite safe in the company of my dog, a mongrel who had adopted me some two months previously.

On arrival at the 'camp', I climbed through the wire fencing and, keeping a good look out, dodged across the open spaces between the thorn bushes. Now and then I caught a glimpse of the birds feeding some distance away.

I had gone about half a mile from the fencing when up started a hare. In an instant my dog gave chase. I tried calling him back, even though I knew it was hopeless. Chasing hares was that dog's passion.

I don't know whether it was the dog's bark or my own shouting, but what I was most anxious to avoid immediately happened. The ostriches were startled and began darting to and fro. Suddenly, I saw a big male bird emerge from a thicket about a hundred yards away. He stood still and stared at me for a few moments. I stared back. Then, expanding his short wings and with his tail erect, he came bounding towards me.

As I had nothing, not even a stick, with which to defend myself, I turned and ran towards the fence. But it was an unequal race. What were my steps of two or three feet against the creature's great strides of sixteen to twenty feet? There was only one hope: to get behind a large bush and try to elude the bird until help came. A dodging game was my only chance.

And so, I rushed for the nearest clump of thorn bushes and waited for my pursuer. The great bird wasted no time—he was immediately upon me.

Then the strangest encounter took place. I dodged this way and that, taking great care not to get directly in front of the ostrich's deadly kick. Ostriches kick forward, and with such terrific force that if you were struck, their huge chisel-like nails would cause you much damage.

I was breathless, and really quite helpless, calling wildly for help as I circled the thorn bush. My strength was ebbing.

How much longer could I keep going? I was ready to drop from exhaustion.

As if aware of my condition, the infuriated bird suddenly doubled back on his course and charged straight at me. With a desperate effort I managed to step to one side. I don't know how, but I found myself holding on to one of the creature's wings, quite close to its body.

It was now the ostrich's turn to be frightened. He began to turn, or rather waltz, moving round and round so quickly that my feet were soon swinging out from his body, almost horizontally! All the while the ostrich kept opening and shutting his beak with loud snaps.

Imagine my situation as I clung desperately to the wing of the enraged bird. He was whirling me round and round as though he were a discus-thrower—and I the discus! My arms soon began to ache with the strain, and the swift and continuous circling was making me dizzy. But I knew that if I relaxed my hold, even for a second, a terrible fate awaited me.

Round and round we went in a great circle. It seemed as if that spiteful bird would never tire. And, I knew I could not hold on much longer. Suddenly, the ostrich went into reverse! This unexpected move made me lose my hold and sent me sprawling to the ground. I landed in a heap near the thorn bush and in an instant, before I even had time to realize what had happened, the big bird was upon me. I thought the end had come. Instinctively, I raised my hands to protect my face. But the ostrich did not strike.

I moved my hands from my face and there stood the creature with one foot raised, ready to deliver a deadly kick! I couldn't move. Was the bird going to play cat-and-mouse with me and prolong the agony?

As I watched, frightened and fascinated, the ostrich turned his head sharply to the left. A second later, he jumped back, turned, and made off as fast as he could go. Dazed, I wondered what had happened to make him beat so unexpected a retreat.

I soon found out. To my great joy, I heard the bark of my truant dog, and the next moment he was jumping around me, licking my face and hands. Needless to say, I returned his caresses most affectionately! And I took good care to see that he did not leave my side until we were well clear of that ostrich 'camp'.

GRANDFATHER'S EARTHQUAKE

'If ever THERE'S a calamity,' Grandmother used to say, 'it will find Grandfather in his bath.' Grandfather loved his bath—which he took in a large round aluminium tub—and sometimes spent as long as an hour in it, 'wallowing' as he called it, and splashing around like a boy.

He was in his bath during the earthquake that convulsed Bengal and Assam on 12 June 1897—an earthquake so severe that even today the region of the great Brahmaputra river basin hasn't settled down. Not long ago it was reported that the entire Shillong plateau had moved an appreciable distance away from the Brahmaputra towards the Bay of Bengal. According to the Geological Survey of India, this shift has been taking place gradually over the past eighty years.

Had Grandfather been alive, he would have added one more clipping to his scrapbook on the earthquake. The clipping goes in anyway, because the scrapbook is now with his children. More than newspaper accounts of the disaster, it was Grandfather's own letters and memoirs that made the earthquake seem recent and vivid; for he, along with Grandmother and two of their children (one of them my father), was living in Shillong, a picturesque little hill station in Assam, when the earth shook and the mountains heaved.

As I have mentioned, Grandfather was in his bath, splashing about, and did not hear the first rumbling. But Grandmother was in the garden, hanging out or taking in the washing (she could never remember which) when, suddenly, the animals began making a hideous noise—a sure intimation of a natural disaster, for animals sense the approach of an earthquake much more quickly than humans.

The crows all took wing, wheeling wildly overhead and cawing loudly. The chickens flapped in circles, as if they were being chased. Two dogs sitting on the veranda suddenly jumped up and ran out with their tails between their legs. Within half a minute of her noticing the noise made by the animals, Grandmother heard a rattling, rumbling noise, like the approach of a train.

The noise increased for about a minute, and then there was the first trembling of the ground. The animals by this time all seemed to have gone mad. Treetops lashed backwards and forwards, doors banged and windows shook, and Grandmother swore later that the house actually swayed in front of her. She had difficulty in standing straight, though this could have been due more to the trembling of her knees than to the trembling of the ground.

The first shock lasted for about a minute and a half. 'I was in my tub having a bath,' Grandfather wrote for posterity, 'which for the first time in the last two months I had taken in the afternoon instead of in the morning. My wife and children and the ayah were downstairs. Then the shock came, accompanied by a loud rumbling sound under the earth and a quaking which increased in intensity every second. It was like putting so many shells in a basket, and shaking them up with a rapid sifting motion from side to side.

'At first I did not realize what it was that caused my tub to sway about and the water to splash. I rose up, and found the earth heaving, while the washstand, basin, ewer, cups and glasses danced and rocked about in the most hideous fashion. I rushed to the inner door to open it and search for wife and children, but could not move the dratted door as boxes, furniture and plaster had come up against it. The back door was the only way of escape. I managed to burst it open, and, thank God, was able to get out. Sections of the thatched roof had slithered down on the four sides like a pack of cards and blocked all the exits and entrances.

'With only a towel wrapped around my waist, I ran out into the open to the front of the house, but found only my wife there. The whole front of the house was blocked by the fallen section of thatch from the roof. Through this I broke my way under the iron railings and extricated the others. The bearer had pluckily borne the weight of the whole thatched roof section on his back as it had slithered down, and in this way saved the ayah and children from being crushed beneath it.'

After the main shock of the earthquake had passed, minor shocks took place at regular intervals of five minutes or so, all through the night. But during that first shake-up the town of Shillong was reduced to ruin and rubble. Everything made of masonry was brought to the ground. Government House, the post office, the jail, all tumbled down. When the jail fell, the prisoners, instead of making their escape, sat huddled on the road waiting for the Superintendent to come to their aid.

'The ground began to heave and shake,' wrote a young girl in a newspaper called *The Englishman*. 'I stayed on my bicycle for a second, and then fell off and got up and tried to run, staggering about from side-to-side of the road. To my left I saw great clouds of dust, which I afterwards discovered to be houses falling and the earth slipping from the sides of the hills. To my right I saw the small dam at the end of the lake torn asunder and the water rushing out, the wooden bridge across the lake break in two and the sides of the lake falling in; and at my feet the ground cracking and opening. I was wild with fear and didn't know which way to turn.'

The lake rose up like a mountain, and then totally disappeared, leaving only a swamp of red mud. Not a house was left standing. People were rushing about, wives looking for husbands, parents looking for children, not knowing whether their loved ones were alive or dead. A crowd of people had collected on the cricket ground, which was considered the safest place; but Grandfather and the family took shelter in a small shop on the road outside his house. The shop was a rickety wooden structure, which had always looked as though it would fall down in a strong wind. But it withstood the earthquake.

And then the rain came and it poured. This was extraordinary, because before the earthquake there wasn't a cloud to be seen; but, five minutes after the shock, Shillong was enveloped in cloud and mist. The shock was felt for more than a hundred miles on the Assam–Bengal Railway. A train was overturned at Shamshernagar; another was derailed at Mantola. Over a thousand people lost their lives in the Cherrapunji Hills, and in other areas, too, the death toll was heavy.

The Brahmaputra burst its banks and many cultivators were drowned in the flood. A tiger was found drowned. And in North Bhagalpur, where the earthquake started, two elephants sat down in the bazaar and refused to get up until the following morning.

Over a hundred men who were at work in Shillong's government printing press were caught in the building when it collapsed, and, though the men of a Gurkha regiment did splendid rescue work, only a few were brought out alive. One of those killed in Shillong was Mr McCabe, a British official.

Grandfather described the ruins of Mr McCabe's house: 'Here a bedpost, there a sword, a broken desk or chair, a bit of torn carpet, a well-known hat with its Indian Civil Service colours, battered books, all speaking reminiscences of the man we mourn.'

While most houses collapsed where they stood, Government House, it seems, 'fell backwards'. The church was a mass of red stones in ugly disorder. The organ was a tortured wreck.

A few days later the family, with other refugees, were making their way to Calcutta to stay with friends or relatives. It was a slow, tedious journey, with many interruptions, for the roads and railway lines had been badly damaged and passengers had often to be transported in trolleys. Grandfather was rather struck at the stoicism displayed by an assistant engineer. At one station a telegram was handed to the engineer informing him that his bungalow had been destroyed. 'Beastly nuisance,' he observed with an aggrieved air. 'I've seen it cave in during a storm, but this is the first time it has played me such a trick on account of an earthquake.'

The family got to Calcutta to find the inhabitants of the capital in a panic; for they too had felt the quake and were expecting it to recur. The damage in Calcutta was slight compared to the devastation elsewhere, but nerves were on edge, and people slept in the open or in carriages. Cracks and fissures had appeared in a number of old buildings, and Grandfather was among the many who were worried at the proposal to fire a salute of sixty guns on Jubilee Day (the Diamond Jubilee of Queen Victoria); they felt the gunfire would bring down a number of shaky buildings. Obviously Grandfather did not wish to be caught in his bath a second time. However, Queen Victoria was not to be deprived of her salute. The guns were duly fired, and Calcutta remained standing.

A TIGER IN THE HOUSE

Timothy, the tiger cub, was discovered by Grandfather on a hunting expedition in the Terai jungle near Dehra.

Grandfather was no shikari, but as he knew the forests of the Siwalik hills better than most people, he was persuaded to accompany the party—it consisted of several Very Important Persons from Delhi—to advise on the terrain and the direction the beaters should take once a tiger had been spotted.

The camp itself was sumptuous—seven large tents (one for each shikari), a dining tent and a number of servants' tents. The dinner was very good, as Grandfather admitted afterwards; it was not often that one saw hot-water plates, finger glasses and seven or eight courses in a tent in the jungle! But that was how things were done in the days of the viceroys... There were also some fifteen elephants, four of them with howdahs for the shikaris, and the others specially trained for taking part in the beat.

The sportsmen never saw a tiger, nor did they shoot anything else, though they saw a number of deer, peacock and wild boar. They were giving up all hope of finding a tiger and were beginning to shoot at jackals, when Grandfather, strolling down the forest path at some distance from the rest of the party, discovered a little tiger about eighteen inches long, hiding among the intricate roots of a banyan tree. Grandfather picked him up and brought him home after the camp had broken up. He had the distinction of being the only member of the party to have bagged any game, dead or alive.

At first the tiger cub, who was named Timothy by Grandmother, was brought up entirely on milk given to him in a feeding bottle by our cook, Mahmoud. But the milk proved too rich for him, and he was put on a diet of raw mutton and cod liver oil, to be followed later by a more tempting diet of pigeons and rabbits.

Timothy was provided with two companions—Toto the monkey, who was bold enough to pull the young tiger by the tail, and then climb up the curtains if Timothy lost his temper; and a small mongrel puppy, found on the road by Grandfather.

At first Timothy appeared to be quite afraid of the puppy and darted back with a spring if it came too near. He would make absurd dashes at it with his large forepaws and then retreat to a ridiculously safe distance. Finally, he allowed the puppy to crawl on his back and rest there!

One of Timothy's favourite amusements was to stalk anyone who would play with him, and so, when I came to live with Grandfather, I became one of the tiger's favourites. With a crafty look in his glittering eyes, and his body crouching, he would creep closer and closer to me, suddenly making a dash for my feet, rolling over on his back and kicking with delight, and pretending to bite my ankles.

He was by this time the size of a full-grown retriever, and when I took him out for walks, people on the road would give us a wide berth. When he pulled hard on his chain, I had difficulty in keeping up with him. His favourite place in the house was the drawing room, and he would make himself comfortable on the long sofa, reclining there with great dignity and snarling at anybody who tried to get him off.

Timothy had clean habits, and would scrub his face with his paws exactly like a cat. At night, he slept in the cook's quarters and was always delighted at being let out by him in the morning.

'One of these days,' declared Grandmother in her prophetic manner, 'we are going to find Timothy sitting on Mahmoud's bed, and no sign of the cook except his clothes and shoes!'

Of course, it never came to that, but when Timothy was about six months old a change came over him; he grew steadily less friendly. When out for a walk with me, he would try to steal away to stalk a cat or someone's pet Pekingese. Sometimes at night we would hear frenzied cackling from the poultry house, and in the morning there would be feathers lying all over the veranda. Timothy had to be chained up more often. And, finally, when he began to stalk Mahmoud about the house with what looked like villainous intent, Grandfather decided it was time to transfer him to a zoo.

The nearest zoo was at Lucknow, two hundred miles away. Reserving a first-class compartment for himself and Timothy—no one would share a compartment with them—Grandfather took him to Lucknow where the zoo authorities were only too glad to receive as a gift a well-fed and fairly civilized tiger.

About six months later, when my grandparents were visiting relatives in Lucknow, Grandfather took the opportunity of calling at the zoo to see how Timothy was getting on. I was not there to accompany him, but I heard all about it when he returned to Dehra.

Arriving at the zoo, Grandfather made straight for the particular cage in which Timothy had been interned. The tiger was there, crouched in a corner, full-grown and with a magnificent striped coat.

'Hello, Timothy!' said Grandfather and, climbing the railing with ease, he put his arm through the bars of the cage.

The tiger approached the bars and allowed Grandfather to put both hands around his head. Grandfather stroked the tiger's forehead and tickled his ear, and, whenever he growled, smacked him across the mouth, which was his old way of keeping him quiet.

He licked Grandfather's hands and only sprang away when a leopard in the next cage snarled at him. Grandfather 'shooed' the leopard away and the tiger returned to lick his hands; but every now and then the leopard would rush at the bars and the tiger would slink back to his corner.

A number of people had gathered to watch the reunion when a keeper pushed his way through the crowd and asked Grandfather what he was doing.

'I'm talking to Timothy,' said Grandfather. 'Weren't you here when I gave him to the zoo six months ago?'

'I haven't been here very long,' said the surprised keeper. 'Please continue your conversation. But I have never been able to touch him myself, he is always very bad tempered.'

'Why don't you put him somewhere else?' suggested Grandfather. 'That leopard keeps frightening him. I'll go and see the superintendent about it.'

Grandfather went in search of the superintendent of the zoo, but found that he had gone home early; and so, after wandering about the zoo for a little while, he returned to Timothy's cage to say goodbye. It was beginning to get dark.

He had been stroking and slapping Timothy for about five minutes when he found another keeper observing him with some alarm. Grandfather recognized him as the keeper who had been there when Timothy had first come to the zoo.

'*You* remember me,' said Grandfather. 'Now why don't you transfer Timothy to another cage, away from this stupid leopard?'

'But... sir...' stammered the keeper, 'it is not your tiger.'

'I know, I know,' said Grandfather testily. 'I realize he is no longer mine. But you might at least take a suggestion or two from me.'

'I remember your tiger very well,' said the keeper. 'He died two months ago.'

'Died!' exclaimed Grandfather.

'Yes, sir, of pneumonia. This tiger was trapped in the hills only last month, and he is very dangerous!'

Grandfather could think of nothing to say. The tiger was still licking his arm, with increasing relish. Grandfather took what seemed to him an age to withdraw his hand from the cage.

With his face near the tiger's he mumbled, 'Goodnight, Timothy,' and giving the keeper a scornful look, walked briskly out of the zoo.

THE OLD GRAMOPHONE

It was a large square mahogany box, well polished, and there was a handle you had to wind, and lids that opened top and front. You changed the steel needle every time you changed the record.

The records were kept flat in a cardboard box to prevent them from warping. If you didn't pack them flat, the heat and humidity turned them into strange shapes which would have made them eligible for an exhibition of modern sculpture.

The winding, the changing of records and needles, the selection of a record were boyhood tasks that I thoroughly enjoyed. I was very methodical in these matters. I hated records being scratched, or the turntable slowing down in the middle of a record, bringing the music of the song to a slow and mournful stop: this happened if the gramophone wasn't fully wound. I was especially careful with my favourites, such as Nelson Eddy singing 'The Mounties' and 'The Hills of Home', various numbers sung by the Ink Spots, and medley of marches.

All this musical activity (requiring much physical exertion on the part of the listener!) took place in a little-known port called Jamnagar, on the west coast of our country, where my father taught English to the young princes and princesses of the state. The gramophone had been installed to amuse me and my mother, but my mother couldn't be bothered with all the effort that went into playing it.

I loved every aspect of the gramophone, even the cleaning of the records with a special cloth. One of my first feats of writing was to catalogue all the records in our collection—only about fifty to begin with—and this cataloguing I did with great care and devotion. My father liked 'grand opera'—Caruso, Gigli and Galli-Curci—but I preferred the lighter ballads of Nelson Eddy, Deanna Durbin, Gracie Fields, Richard Tauber, and 'The Street Singer' (Arthur Tracy). It may seem incongruous, to have been living within sound of the Arabian Sea and listening to Nelson sing most beautifully of the mighty Missouri river, but it was perfectly natural to me. I grew up with that music, and I love it still.

I was a lonely boy, without friends of my own age, so that the gramophone and the record collection meant a lot to me. My catalogue went into new and longer editions, taking in the names of composers, lyricists and accompanists.

When we left Jamnagar, the gramophone accompanied us on the long train journey (three days and three nights, with several changes) to Dehradun. Here, in the spacious grounds of my grandparents' home at the foothills of the Himalayas, songs like 'The Hills of Home' and 'Shenandoah' did not seem out of place.

Grandfather had a smaller gramophone and a record collection of his own. His tastes were more 'modern' than mine. Dance music was his passion, and there were any number of foxtrots, tangos and beguines played by the leading dance bands of the 1940s. Granny preferred waltzes and taught me to waltz. I would waltz with her on the broad veranda, to the strains of 'The Blue Danube' and 'The Skater's Waltz', while a soft breeze rustled in the banana fronds. I became quite good at the waltz, but then I saw Gene Kelly tap-dancing in a brash, colourful

MGM musical, and—base treachery!—forsook the waltz and began tap-dancing all over the house, much to Granny's dismay.

All this is pure nostalgia, of course, but why be ashamed of it? Nostalgia is simply an attempt to try and preserve that which was good in the past... The past has served us. Why not serve the past in this way?

When I was sent to boarding school and was away from home for nine long months, I really missed the gramophone. How I looked forward to coming home for the winter holidays! There were, of course, some new records waiting for me. And Grandfather had taken to the Brazilian rumba, which was all the rage just then. Yes, Grandfather did the rumba with great aplomb.

I believe he moved on to the samba and then the calypso, but by then I'd left India and was away for five years. A great deal had changed in my absence. My grandparents had moved on, and my mother had sold the old gramophone and replaced it with a large radiogram. But this wasn't so much fun: I wanted something I could wind!

I keep hoping our old gramophone will turn up somewhere—maybe in an antique shop or in someone's attic or storeroom, or at a sale. Then I shall buy it back, whatever the cost, and install it in my study and have the time of my life winding it up and playing the old records. I now have tapes of some of them, but that won't stop me listening to the gramophone. I have even kept a box of needles in readiness for the great day.

THE GARDEN OF MEMORIES

Sitting in the sun on a winter's afternoon, feeling my age just a little (I'm over seventy), I began reminiscing about my boyhood in the Dehra of long ago, and found myself missing the old times—friends of my youth, my grandmother, our neighbours, interesting characters in our small town, and, of course, my eccentric relative—the dashing young Uncle Ken!

Yes, Dehra was a small town then—uncluttered, uncrowded, with quiet lanes and pretty gardens and shady orchards.

The only time in my life that I was fortunate enough to live in a house with a real garden—as opposed to a backyard or balcony or windswept veranda—during those three years when I spent my winter holidays (December to March) in Granny's bungalow on Old Survey Road.

The best months were February and March, when the garden was heavy with the scent of sweet peas, the flower beds were a many-coloured quilt of phlox, antirrhinum, larkspur, petunia and Californian poppy. I loved the bright yellows of the Californian poppies, the soft pinks of our own Indian poppies, the subtle perfume of petunias and snapdragons and, above all, the delicious, overpowering scent of the massed sweet peas, which grew taller than me.

Flowers made a sensualist of me. They taught me the delight of smell, colour and touch—yes, touch too, for to press a rose to one's lips is much like a gentle, hesitant, exploratory kiss...

THE GARDEN OF MEMORIES

Granny decided on what flowers should be sown, and where. Dhuki, the gardener, did the digging and weeding, sowing and transplanting. He was a skinny, taciturn old man, who had begun to resemble the weeds he flung away. He did not mind answering my questions, but never did he allow our brief conversations to interfere with his work. Most of the time he was to be found on his haunches, hoeing and weeding with a little spade called a *kburpi*. He would throw out the smaller marigolds because he said Granny did not care for them. I felt sorry for these colourful little discards, collected them and transplanted them to a little garden patch of my own at the back of the house, near the garden wall.

Another so-called weed that I liked was a little purple flower that grew in clusters all over Dehra, on any bit of wasteland, in ditches, on canal banks. It flowered from late winter into early summer, and it will be growing in the valley and beyond long after gardens have become obsolete, as indeed they must, considering the rapid spread of urban clutter. It brightens up fields and roads where you least expect a little colour. I have since learnt that it is called ageratum, and that it is actually prized as a garden (lower in Europe, -where it is described as Blue Mink in the seed catalogues. Here it isn't blue but purple, and it grows all the way from Rajpur (just above Dehra) to the outskirts of Meerut; then it disappears.

Other garden outcasts include the lantana bush—an attractive wayside shrub—the thorn apple, various thistles, daisies and dandelions. But both Granny and Dhuki had declared a war on weeds, and many of these commoners had to exist outside the confines of the garden. Like slum children, they survived rather well in ditches and on the roadside, while their more pampered fellow citizens were prone to leaf diseases and parasitic infections of various kinds.

The veranda was a place where Granny herself could potter about, attending to various ferns, potted palms and colourful geraniums. She averred that geraniums kept snakes away, although she never said why. As far as I know, snakes don't have a great sense of smell.

One day, I saw a snake curled up at the bottom of the veranda steps. When it saw me, or became aware of my footsteps, it uncoiled itself and slithered away. I told Granny about it, and observed that it did not seem to be bothered by the geraniums.

'Ah,' said Granny. 'But for those geraniums, the snake would have entered the house!' There was no arguing with Granny. Or with Uncle Ken, when he was at his most pontifical.

One day, while walking near the canal bank, we came upon a green grass snake holding a frog in its mouth. The frog was half in, half out, and with the help of my hockey stick, I made the snake disgorge the unfortunate creature. It hopped away, none the worse for its adventure.

I felt quite pleased with myself. 'Is this what it feels like to be God?' I mused aloud.

'No,' said Uncle Ken. 'God would have let the snake finish its lunch.'

Uncle Ken was one of those people who went through life without having to do much, although a great deal seemed to happen around him. He acted as a sort of catalyst for events that involved the family, friends, neighbours, the town itself. He believed in the fruits of hard work: other people's hard work,

Ken was good-looking as a boy, and his sisters (including my mother, the youngest) doted on him. He took full advantage of their devotion, and, as the girls grew up and married, Ken took it for granted that they and their husbands would continue to look after his welfare. You could say he was the originator of the welfare state: his own.

I'll say this for Uncle Ken, he had a large fund of curiosity in his nature, and he loved to explore the town we lived in, and any other town or city where he might happen to find himself. With one sister settled in Lucknow, another in Ranchi, a third in Bhopal and a fourth in Simla, Uncle Ken managed to see a cross section of India by dividing his time between all his sisters and their long-suffering husbands.

Uncle Ken liked to walk. Occasionally he borrowed my bicycle, but he had a tendency to veer off the main road and into ditches and other obstacles. After a collision with a bullock cart, in which he tore his trousers and damaged the handlebar of my bicycle, he concluded that walking was the best way of getting around Dehra.

Uncle Ken dressed quite smartly for a man of no particular occupation. He had a blue striped blazer and a red striped blazer; he usually wore white or off-white trousers, immaculately pressed (by Granny). He was the delight of shoeshine boys, for he would always have his shoes polished. Summers he wore a straw hat, telling everyone he had worn it for the Varsity Boat Race while rowing for Oxford (he hadn't attended college there, let alone rowed for the college team); winters he wore one of Grandfather's old felt hats. He seldom went bareheaded. At thirty he was almost completely bald, prompting Aunt Mabel to remark, 'Well, Ken, you must be grateful for small mercies. At least you'll never have bats getting entangled in your hair.'

Thanks to all his walking, Uncle Ken had a good digestion, which kept pace with a hearty appetite. Our walks would be punctuated by short stops at chaat shops, sweet shops, fruit stalls, confectioners, small bakeries and other eateries.

'Have you brought any pocket money along?' he would ask, for he was usually broke.

'Granny gave me five rupees.'

'We'll try some rasgullas, then.'

And the rasgullas would be followed by gulab jamuns, until my five rupees were finished. Uncle Ken received a small allowance from Granny, but he ferreted it away to spend on clothes, preferring to spend my pocket money on perishables such as ice creams, kulfis and Indian sweets.

On one occasion, when neither of us had any money, Uncle Ken decided to venture into a sugarcane field on the outskirts of the town. He had broken off a stick of cane, and was busy chewing on it, when the owner of the field spotted us and let out a volley of imprecations. We fled from the field, with the irate farmer giving chase. I could run faster than Uncle Ken, and did so. The farmer would have caught up with Uncle Ken if the latter's hat hadn't blown off, causing a diversion. The farmer picked up the hat, examined it, seemed to fancy it, and put it on. Several small boys clapped and cheered. The farmer marched off, wearing the hat, and Uncle Ken wisely decided against making any attempt to retrieve it.

'I'll get another one,' he said philosophically.

He wore a pith helmet, or sola topi, for the next few days, as he thought it would protect him from sticks and stones. For a while he harboured a paranoia that all the sugarcane farmers in the valley were looking for him, to avenge his foray into their fields. But after some time he discarded the topi because, according to him, it interfered with his good looks.

Granny grew the best sweet peas in Dehra. But she never entered them at the Annual Flower Show held every year in the second week of March. She did not grow flowers to win prizes, she said; she grew them to please the spirit of Grandfather, who still hovered about the house and grounds he'd built thirty years earlier.

Miss Kellner, Granny's crippled but valued tenant, said the flowers were grown to attract beautiful butterflies, and she was right. In early summer, swarms of butterflies flitted about the garden.

Uncle Ken had no compunction about winning prizes, even though he did nothing to deserve them. Without telling anyone, he submitted a large display of Granny's sweet peas for the flower show, and when the prizes were announced, lo and behold, Kenneth Clerke had been awarded first prize for his magnificent display of sweet peas.

Granny refused to speak to him for several days.

Uncle Ken had been hoping for a cash prize, but they gave him a flower vase. He told me it was a Ming vase. But it looked more like Meerut to me. He offered it to Granny, hoping to propitiate her; but, still displeased with him, she gave it to Mr Khastgir, the artist next door, who kept his paintbrushes in it.

Although I was sometimes a stubborn and unruly boy (my hero was Richmal Crompton's William), I got on well with old ladies, especially those who, like Miss Kellner, were fond of offering me chocolates, marzipans, soft nankhatai biscuits (made at Yusuf's bakery in the Dilaram Bazaar), and pieces of crystallized ginger. Miss Kellner couldn't walk—had never walked—and so she could only admire the garden from a distance, but it was from her that I learnt the names of many flowers, trees, birds and even butterflies.

Uncle Ken wasn't any good with names, but he wanted to catch a rare butterfly. He said he could make a fortune if he caught a leaf butterfly called the Purple Emperor. He equipped himself with a butterfly net, a bottle of ether, and a cabinet for mounting his trophies; he then prowled all over the grounds, making frequent forays at anything that flew.

He caught several common species—Red Admirals, a Tortoiseshell, a Painted Lad, even the occasional dragonfly—but the high-flying Purple Emperor and other exotics eluded him, as did the fortune he was always aspiring to make.

Eventually he caught an angry wasp, which stung him through the netting. Chased by its fellow wasps, he took refuge in the lily pond and emerged sometime later, draped in lilies and waterweeds.

After this, Uncle Ken retired from the butterfly business, insisting that tiger hunting was safer.

LIFE WITH UNCLE KEN

Granny's Fabulous Kitchen

As kitchens went, it wasn't all that big. It wasn't as big as the bedroom or the living room, but it was big enough, and there was a pantry next to it. What made it fabulous was all that came out of it: good things to eat, like cakes and curries, chocolate fudge and peanut toffee, jellies and jam tarts, meat pies, stuffed turkeys, stuffed chickens, stuffed eggplants, and hams stuffed with stuffed chickens.

As far as I was concerned, Granny was the best cook in the whole wide world.

Two generations of Clerkes had lived in India and my maternal grandmother had settled in a small town in the foothills, just where the great plain ended and the Himalayas began. The town was called Dehradun. It's still there, though much bigger and busier now. Granny had a house—a large, rambling bungalow—on the outskirts of the town, on Old Survey Road. In the grounds were many trees, most of them fruit trees. Mangoes, litchis, guavas, bananas, papayas, lemons—there was room for all of them, including a giant jackfruit tree casting its shadow on the walls of the house.

> Blessed is the house upon whose walls
> The shade of an old tree softly falls.

I remember those lines of Granny's. They were true words, because it was a good house to live in, especially for a nine-year-old with a tremendous appetite. If Granny was the best cook in the world, I must have been the boy with the best appetite.

Every winter, when I came home from boarding school, I would spend about a month with Granny, before going on to spend the rest of the holidays with my mother and stepfather. My parents couldn't cook. They employed a khansama—a professional cook—who made a good mutton curry but little else. Mutton curry for lunch and mutton curry for dinner can be a bit tiring, especially for a boy who liked to eat almost everything.

Granny was glad to have me because she lived alone most of the time. Not entirely alone, though... There was a gardener, Dhuki, who lived in an outhouse. And he had a son called Mohan, who was about my age. And there was Ayah, an elderly maidservant, who helped with the household work. And there was a Siamese cat with bright blue eyes, and a mongrel dog called Crazy, because he ran circles round the house.

And, of course, there was Uncle Ken, Granny's only son, who came to stay whenever he was out of a job (which was quite often) or when he felt like enjoying some of Granny's cooking.

So Granny wasn't really alone. All the same, she was glad to have me. She didn't enjoy cooking for herself, she said; she had to cook for *someone*. And although the cat and the dog, and sometimes Uncle Ken, appreciated her efforts, a good cook likes to have a boy to feed, because boys are adventurous and ready to try the most unusual dishes.

Whenever Granny tried out a new recipe on me, she would wait for my comments and reactions, and then make a note in one of her exercise books. These notes were useful when she made the dish again, or when she tried it out on others.

'Do you like it?' she'd ask, after I'd taken a few mouthfuls.

'Yes, Gran.'

'Sweet enough.'

'Yes, Gran.'

'Not *too* sweet.'

'No, Gran.'

'Wouldyou like some more?'

'Yes, please, Gran.'

'Well, finish it off.'

'If you say so, Gran.'

Roast duck. This was one of Granny's specials. The first time I had roast duck at Granny's place, Uncle Ken was there too.

He'd just lost a job as a railway guard, and had come to stay with Granny until he could find another job. He always stayed as long as he could, only moving on when Granny offered to get him a job as an assistant master in Padre Lai's Academy for Small Boys. Uncle Ken couldn't stand small boys. They made him nervous, he said. I made him nervous too, but there was only one of me, and there was always Granny to protect him. At Padre Lai's, there were over a hundred small boys.

Although Uncle Ken had a tremendous appetite, and ate just as much as I did, he never praised Granny's dishes. I think this is why I was annoyed with him at times, and why, sometimes, I enjoyed making him feel nervous.

Uncle Ken looked down at the roast duck, his glasses slipping down to the edge of his nose.

'Hmm... Duck again?'

'What do you mean, duck again? You haven't had duck since you were here last month,' retorted Granny.

'That's what I mean,' said Uncle Ken. 'Somehow, one expects more variety from you.'

All the same, he took two large helpings and ate most of the stuffing before I could get at it. I took my revenge by emptying all the apple sauce on to my plate. Uncle Ken knew I loved the stuffing; and I knew he was crazy about Granny's apple sauce. So we were even.

'When are you joining your parents?' he asked hopefully, over the jam tart.

'I may not go to them this year,' I said. 'When are you getting another job, Uncle?'

'Oh, I'm thinking of taking rest for a couple of months.'

I enjoyed helping Granny and Ayah with the washing up. While we were at work, Uncle Ken would take a siesta on the veranda or switch on the radio to listen to dance music. Glenn Miller and his swing band was all the rage then.

'And how do you like your Uncle Ken?' asked Granny one day, as she emptied the bones from his plate into the dog's bowl.

'I wish he was someone else's uncle,' I said.

'He's not so bad, really. Just eccentric.'

'What's eccentric?'

'Oh, just a little crazy.'

'At least Crazy runs round the house,' I said. 'I've never seen Uncle Ken running.'

But I did one day.

Mohan and I were playing marbles in the shade of the mango grove when we were taken aback by the sight of Uncle Ken charging across the compound, pursued by a swarm of bees. He'd been smoking a cigar under a silk-cotton tree, and the fumes had disturbed the wild bees in their hive, directly above him. Uncle Ken fled indoors and leapt into a tub of cold water. He had received a few stings and decided to remain in bed for three days. Ayah took his meals to him on a tray.

'I didn't know Uncle Ken could run so fast,' I said later that day.

'It's nature's way of compensating,' said Granny.

'What's compensating?'

'Making up for things... Now at least Uncle Ken knows that he can run. Isn't that wonderful?'

♦

Whenever Granny made vanilla or chocolate fudge, she gave me some to take to Mohan, the gardener's son. It was no use taking him roast duck or curried chicken because in his house no one ate meat. But Mohan liked sweets—Indian sweets, which were made with lots of milk and lots of sugar, as well as Granny's home-made English sweets.

We would climb into the branches of the jackfruit tree and eat fudge or peppermints or sticky toffee. We couldn't eat the jackfruit, except when it was cooked as a vegetable or made into a pickle. But the tree itself was wonderful for climbing. And some wonderful creatures lived in it—squirrels and fruit bats and a pair of green parrots. The squirrels were friendly and soon got into the habit of eating from our hands. They, too, were fond of chocolate fudge. One young squirrel would even explore my pockets to see if I was keeping anything from him.

Mohan and I could climb almost any tree in the garden, and if Granny was looking for us, she'd call from the front veranda and then from the back veranda and then from the pantry at the side of the house and, Finally, from the bathroom window on the other side of the house. There were trees on all sides and it was impossible to tell which one we were in, until we answered her call. Sometimes Crazy would give us away by barking beneath our tree.

When there was fruit to be picked, Mohan did the picking. The mangoes and litchis came into season

During the summer, I was away at boarding school, so I couldn't help with the fruit gathering. The papayas were in season during the winter, but you don't climb papaya trees; they are too slender and wobbly. You knock the papayas down with a long pole.

Mohan also helped Granny with the pickling. She was justly famous for her pickles. Green mangoes, pickled in oil, were always popular. So was her hot lime pickle. And she was equally good at pickling turnips, carrots, cauliflowers, chillies and other fruits and vegetables. She could pickle almost anything, from a nasturtium seed to a jackfruit. Uncle Ken didn't care for pickles, so I was always urging Granny to make more of them.

My own preference was for sweet chutneys and sauces, but I ate pickles too, even the very hot ones.

One winter, when Granny's funds were low, Mohan and I went from house to house, selling pickles for her.

In spite of all the people and pets she fed, Granny wasn't rich. The house had come to her from Grandfather, but there wasn't much money in the bank. The mango crop brought in a fair amount every year, and there was a small pension from the railways (Grandfather had been one of the pioneers who'd helped bring the railway line to Dehra at the turn of the century), but there was no other income. And now that I come to think of it, all those wonderful meals consisted only of the one course, followed by a sweet dish. It was Granny's cooking that turned a modest meal into a feast.

I wasn't ashamed to sell pickles for Granny. It was great fun. Mohan and I armed ourselves with baskets filled with pickle bottles, then set off to cover all the houses in our area.

Major Wilkie, across the road, was our first customer. He had a red beard and bright blue eyes and was almost always good-humoured.

'And what have you got there, young Bond?' he asked.

'Pickle, sir.'

'Pickles! Have you been making them?'

'No, sir, they're my grandmother's. We're selling them, so we can buy a turkey for Christmas.'

'Mrs Clerke's pickles, eh? Well, I'm glad mine is the first house on your way, because I'm sure that basket will soon be empty. There is no one who can make a pickle like your grandmother, son. I've said it before and I'll say it again, she's God's gift to a world that's terribly short of good cooks. My wife's gone shopping, so I can talk quite freely, you see... What have you got this time? Stuffed chillies, I trust. She knows they're my favourite. I shall be deeply wounded if there are no stuffed chillies in the basket.'

There were, in fact, three bottles of stuffed red chillies in the basket, and Major Wilkie took all of them.

Our next call was at Miss Kellner's house. Miss Kellner couldn't eat hot food, so it was no use offering her pickles. But she bought a bottle of preserved ginger. And she gave me a little prayer book. Whenever I went to see her, she gave me a new prayer book. Soon I had quite a collection of prayer books. What was I to do with them? Finally, Uncle Ken took them off me, and sold them back to Miss Kellner.

Further down the road, Dr Dutt, who was in charge of the hospital, bought several bottles of lime pickle, saying it was good for his liver. And Mr Hari, who owned a garage at the end of the road and sold all the latest cars, bought two bottles of pickled onions and begged us to bring him another two the following month.

By the time we got home, the basket would usually be empty and Granny richer by twenty or thirty rupees—enough, in those days, for a turkey.

'It's high time you found a job,' said Granny to Uncle Ken one day.

'There are no jobs in Dehra,' complained Uncle Ken.

'How can you tell? You've never looked for one. And anyway, you don't have to stay here forever. Your sister Emily is headmistress of a school in Lucknow. You could go to her. She said before that she was ready to put you in charge of a dormitory.'

'Bah!' said Uncle Ken. 'Honestly, you don't expect me to look after a dormitory seething with forty or fifty demented small boys?'

'What's demented?' I asked.

'Shut up,' said Uncle Ken.

'It means crazy,' said Granny.

'So many words mean crazy,' I complained. 'Why don't we just say crazy? We have a crazy dog, and now Uncle Ken is crazy too.'

Uncle Ken clipped me over my ear, and Granny said, 'Your uncle isn't crazy, so don't be disrespectful. He's just lazy.'

'And eccentric,' I said. 'I heard he was eccentric.'

'Who said I was eccentric?' demanded Uncle Ken.

'Miss Leslie,' I lied. I knew Uncle Ken was fond of Miss Leslie, who ran a beauty parlour in Dehra's smart shopping centre, Astley Hall.

'I don't believe you,' said Uncle Ken. 'Anyway, when did you see Miss Leslie?'

'We sold her a bottle of mint chutney last week. I told her you liked mint chutney. But she said she'd bought it for Mr Brown, who's taking her to the pictures tomorrow.'

'Eat well, but don't overeat,' Granny used to tell me. 'Good food is a gift from God, and like any other gift, it can be misused.'

She'd made a list of kitchen proverbs and pinned it to the pantry door—not so high that I couldn't read it, either. These were some of the proverbs:

Light suppers make long lives.
Better a small fish than an empty dish.
There is skill in all things, even in making porridge.
Eating and drinking should not keep men from thinking.
Dry bread at home is better than roast meat abroad.
A good dinner sharpens the wit and softens the heart.
Let not your tongue cut your throat.

Uncle Ken Does Nothing

To our surprise, Uncle Ken got a part-time job as a guide, showing tourists the 'sights' around Dehra.

There was an old fort near the riverbed; and a seventeenth-century temple; and a jail where Pandit Nehru had spent some time as a political prisoner; and, about ten miles into the foothills, the hot sulphur springs.

Uncle Ken told us he was taking a parry of six American tourists—husbands and wives—to the sulphur springs. Granny was pleased. Uncle Ken was busy at last! She gave him a hamper filled with ham sandwiches, home-made biscuits and a dozen oranges—ample provision for a day's outing.

The sulphur springs were only ten miles from Dehra, but we didn't see Uncle Ken for three days.

He was a sight when he got back. His clothes were dusty

and torn; his cheeks were sunken; and the little bald patch on top of his head had been burnt a bright red.

'What have you been doing to yourself?' asked Granny.

Uncle Ken sank into the armchair on the veranda. 'I'm starving, Mother. Give me something to eat.'

'What happened to the food you took with you?'

'There were seven of us, and it was all finished on the first day.'

'Well, it was only supposed to last a day. You said you were going to the sulphur springs.'

'Yes, that's where we were going,' said Uncle Ken. 'But we never reached them. We got lost in the hills.'

'How could you possibly have got lost in the hills? You had only to walk straight along the riverbed and up the valley . . . You ought to know; you were the guide and you'd been there before, when your father was alive.'

'Yes, I know,' said Uncle Ken, looking crestfallen. 'But I forgot the way. That is, I forgot the valley. I mean, I took them up the wrong valley. And I kept thinking the springs would be at the same river, but it wasn't the same river... So we kept walking, until we were in the hills, and then I looked down and saw we'd come up the wrong valley. We had to spend the night under the stars. It was very, very cold. And next day I thought we'd come back a quicker way, through Mussoorie, but we took the wrong path and reached Kempti instead... And then we walked down to the motor road and caught a bus.'

I helped Granny put Uncle Ken to bed, and then helped her make him a strengthening onion soup. I took him the soup on a tray, and he made a face while drinking it and then asked for more. He was in bed for two days, while Ayah and I took turns taking him his meals. He wasn't a bit grateful.

♦

When Uncle Ken complained he was losing his hair and that his bald patch was increasing in size, Granny looked up her book of old recipes and said there was one for baldness, which Grandfather had used with great success. It consisted of a lotion made with gherkins soaked in brandy. Uncle Ken said he'd try it.

Granny soaked some gherkins in brandy for a week, then gave the bottle to Uncle Ken with instructions to rub a little into his scalp mornings and evenings.

Next day, when she looked into his room, she found only gherkins in the bottle. Uncle Ken had drunk all the brandy.

♦

Uncle Ken liked to whistle. Hands in his pockets, nothing to do, he would stroll about the house, around the garden, up and down the road, whistling feebly to himself.

It was always the same whistle, tuneless to everyone except my uncle.

'What are you whistling today, Uncle Ken?' I'd ask.

'"Ol' Man River". Don't you recognize it?'

And the next time around he'd be whistling the same notes, and I'd say, 'Still whistling "Ol' Man River", Uncle?'

'No, I'm not. This is "Danny Boy". Can't you tell the difference?'

And he'd slouch off, whistling tunelessly. Sometimes it irritated Granny.

'Can't you stop whistling, Ken? It gets on my nerves. Why don't you try singing for a change?'

'I can't. It's "The Blue Danube"; there aren't any words.' And he'd waltz around the kitchen, whistling.

'Well, you can do your whistling and waltzing on the

veranda,' Granny would say. 'I won't have it in the kitchen. It spoils the food.'

When Uncle Ken had a bad tooth removed by our dentist, Dr Kapadia, we thought his whistling would stop. But it only became louder and shriller.

One day, while he was strolling along the road, hands in his pockets, doing nothing, whistling very loudly, a girl on a bicycle passed him. She stopped suddenly, got off the bicycle, and blocked his way.

'If you whistle at me every time I pass, Kenneth Clerke,' she said, 'I'll wallop you!'

Uncle Ken went red in the face. 'I wasn't whistling at you,' he said.

'Well, I don't see anyone else on the road.'

'I was whistling "God Save the King". Don't you recognize it?'

Uncle Ken on the Job

'We'll have to do something about Uncle Ken,' said Granny to the world at large.

I was in the kitchen with her, shelling peas and popping a few into my mouth now and then. Suzie, the Siamese cat, sat on the sideboard, patiently watching Granny prepare an Irish stew. Suzie liked Irish stew.

'It's not that I mind him staying,' said Granny, 'and I don't want any money from him, either. But it isn't healthy for a young man to remain idle for so long.'

'Is Uncle Ken a young man, Gran?'

'He's thirty. Everyone says he'll improve as he grows up.'

'He could go and live with Aunt Mabel.'

'He *does* go and live with Aunt Mabel. He also lives with Aunt Emily and Aunt Beryl. That's his trouble—he has too many doting sisters ready to put him up and put up with him ...Their husbands are all quite well off and can afford to have him now and then. So our Ken spends three months with Mabel, three months with Beryl, three months with me. That way he gets by as everyone's guest and doesn't have to worry about making a living.'

'He's lucky in a way,' I said.

'His luck won't last forever. Already Mabel is talking of going to New Zealand. And once India is free—in just a year or two from now—Emily and Beryl will probably go off to England, because their husbands are in the army and all the British officers will be leaving.'

'Can't Uncle Ken follow them to England?'

'He knows he'll have to start working if he goes there. When your aunts find they have to manage without servants, they won't be ready to keep Ken for long periods. In any case, who's going to pay his fare to England or New Zealand?'

'If he can't go, he'll stay here with you, Granny. You'll be here, won't you?'

'Not forever. Only while I live.'

'You won't go to England?'

'No, I've grown up here. I'm like the trees. I've taken root, I won't be going away—not until, like an old tree, I'm without any more leaves... You'll go, though, when you are bigger. You'll probably finish your schooling abroad.'

'I'd rather finish it here. I want to spend all my holidays with you. If I go away, who'll look after you when you grow old?'

'I'm old already. Over sixty.'

'Is that very old? It's only a little older than Uncle Ken.

And how will you look after him when you're *really* old?'

'He can look after himself if he tries. And it's time he started. It's time he took a job.'

I pondered over the problem. I could think of nothing that would suit Uncle Ken—or rather, I could think of no one who would find him suitable. It was Ayah who made a suggestion.

'The Maharani of Jetpur needs a tutor for her children,' she said. 'Just a boy and a girl.'

'How do you know?' asked Granny.

'I heard it from their ayah. The pay is 200 rupees a month, and there is not much work—only two hours every morning.'

'That should suit Uncle Ken,' I said.

'Yes, it's a good idea,' said Granny. 'We'll have to talk him into applying. He ought to go over and see them. The Maharani is a good person to work for.'

Uncle Ken agreed to go over and inquire about the job. The Maharani was out when he called, but he was interviewed by the Maharaja.

'Do you play tennis?' asked the Maharaja.

'Yes,' said Uncle Ken, who remembered having played a bit of tennis when he was a schoolboy.

'In that case, the job's yours. I've been looking for a fourth player for a doubles match... By the way, were you at Cambridge?'

'No, I was at Oxford,' said Uncle Ken.

The Maharaja was impressed. An Oxford man who could play tennis was just the sort of tutor he wanted for his children.

When Uncle Ken told Granny about the interview, she said, 'But you haven't been to Oxford, Ken. How could you say that!'

'Of course I have been to Oxford. Don't you remember? I spent two years there with your brother Jim!'

'Yes, but you were helping him in his pub in the town. You weren't at the university.'

'Well, the Maharaja never asked me if I had been to the university. He asked me if I was at Cambridge, and I said no, I was at Oxford, which was perfectly true. He didn't ask me what I was doing at Oxford. What difference does it make?'

And he strolled off, whistling.

◆

To our surprise, Uncle Ken was a great success at his job. In the beginning, anyway.

The Maharaja was such a poor tennis player that he was delighted to discover that there was someone who was even worse. So, instead of becoming a doubles partner for the Maharaja, Uncle Ken became his favourite singles opponent. As long as he could keep losing to His Highness, Uncle Ken's job was safe.

In between tennis matches and accompanying his employer on duck shoots, Uncle Ken squeezed in a few lessons for the children, teaching them reading, writing and arithmetic. Sometimes he took me along, so that I could tell him when he got his sums wrong. Uncle Ken wasn't very good at subtraction, although he could add fairly well.

The Maharaja's children were smaller than me. Uncle Ken would leave me with them, saying, 'Just see that they do their sums properly, Ruskin,' and he would stroll off to the tennis courts, hands in his pockets, whistling tunelessly.

Even if his pupils had different answers to the same sum, he would give both of them an encouraging pat, saying, 'Excellent, excellent. I'm glad to see both of you trying so hard. One of you is right and one of you is wrong, but as I don't want to discourage either of you, I won't say who's right and who's wrong!'

But afterwards, on the way home, he'd ask me, 'Which was the right answer, Ruskin?'

Uncle Ken always maintained that he would never have lost his job if he hadn't beaten the Maharaja at tennis.

Not that Uncle Ken had any intention of winning. But by playing occasional games with the Maharaja's secretaries and guests, his tennis had improved and so, try as hard as he might to lose, he couldn't help winning a match against his employer.

The Maharaja was furious.

'Mr Clerke,' he said sternly, 'I don't think you realize the importance of losing. We can't all win, you know. Where would the world be without losers?'

'I'm terribly sorry,' said Uncle Ken. 'It was just a fluke, Your Highness.'

The Maharaja accepted Uncle Ken's apologies; but a week later it happened again. Kenneth Clerke won and the Maharaja stormed off the court without saying a word. The following day he turned up at lesson time. As usual, Uncle Ken and the children were engaged in a game of noughts and crosses.

'We won't be requiring your services from tomorrow, Mr Clerke. I've asked my secretary to give you a month's salary in lieu of notice.'

Uncle Ken came home with his hands in his pockets, whistling cheerfully.

'You're early,' said Granny.

'They don't need me any more,' said Uncle Ken.

'Oh, well, never mind. Come in and have your tea.'

Granny must have known the job wouldn't last very long. And she wasn't one to nag. As she said later, 'At least he tried. And it lasted longer than most of his jobs—two months.'

Uncle Ken at the Wheel

On my next visit to Dehra, Mohan met me at the station. We got into a tonga with my luggage and we went rattling and jingling along Dehra's quiet roads to Granny's house.

'Tell me all the news, Mohan.'

'Not much to tell. Some of the sahibs are selling their houses and going away. Suzie has had kittens.' Granny knew I'd been in the train for two nights, and she had a huge breakfast ready for me. Porridge, scrambled eggs on toast. Bacon with fried tomatoes. Toast and marmalade. Sweet milky tea.

She told me there'd been a letter from Uncle Ken.

'He says he's the assistant manager at Firpo's hotel in Simla,' she said. 'The salary is very good, and he gets free board and lodging. It's a steady job and I hope he keeps it.'

Three days later Uncle Ken was on the veranda steps with his bedding roll and battered suitcase.

'Have you given up the hotel job?' asked Granny.

'No,' said Uncle Ken. 'They have closed down.'

'I hope it wasn't because of you.'

'No, Mother. The bigger hotels in the hill stations are all closing down.'

'Well, never mind. Come along and have your tiffin. There is a kofta curry today. It's Ruskin's favourite.'

'Oh, is he here too? I have far too many nephews and nieces. Still, he's preferable to those two girls of Mabel's. They made life miserable for me all the time I was with them in Simla.'

Over tiffin (as lunch was called in those days), Uncle Ken talked very seriously about ways and means of earning a living.

'There is only one taxi in the whole of Dehra,' he mused.

'Surely there is business for another?'*

'I'm sure there is,' said Granny. 'But where does it get you? In the first place, you don't have a taxi. And in the second place, you can't drive.'

'I can soon learn. There's a driving school in town. And I can use Dad's old car. It's been gathering dust in the garage for years.' (He was referring to Grandfather's vintage Hillman Roadster. It was a 1926 model: about twenty years old.)

'I don't think it will run now,' said Granny.

'Of course it will. It just needs some oiling and greasing and a spot of paint.'

'All right, learn to drive. Then we will see about the Roadster.'

So Uncle Ken joined the driving school.

He was very regular, going for his lessons for an hour in the evening. Granny paid the fee.

After a month, Uncle Ken announced that he could drive and that he was taking the Roadster out for a trial run.

'You haven't got your licence yet,' said Granny.

'Oh, I won't take her far,' said Uncle Ken. 'Just down the road and back again.'

He spent all morning cleaning the car. Granny gave him money for a can of petrol.

After tea, Uncle Ken said, 'Come along, Ruskin, hop in and I will give you a ride. Bring Mohan along too.'

Mohan and I needed no urging. We got into the car beside Uncle Ken.

'Now don't go too fast, Ken,' said Granny anxiously. 'You are not used to the car as yet.'

---

*In the early 1940s, Dehra had only one or two taxis. Today, there are over 500 plying in the town.

Uncle Ken nodded and smiled and gave two sharp toots on the horn. He was feeling pleased with himself.

Driving through the gate, he nearly ran over Crazy.

Miss Kellner, who was carried out to the rickshaw for her evening ride, saw Uncle Ken at the wheel of the Roadster and begged to be taken indoors.

Uncle Ken drove straight and fast, tooting the horn without a break.

At the end of the road there was a roundabout.

'We'll turn here,' said Uncle Ken, 'and then drive back again.'

He turned the steering wheel; we began going round the roundabout; but the steering wheel wouldn't turn all the way, not as much as Uncle Ken would have liked it to... So, instead of going round, we took a right turn and kept going, straight on and through the Maharaja of Jetpur's garden wall!

It was a single-brick wall, and the Roadster knocked it down and emerged on the other side without any damage to the car or any of its occupants. Uncle Ken brought it to a halt in the middle of the Maharaja's lawn.

Running across the grass came the Maharaja himself, flanked by his secretaries and their assistants.

When he saw that it was Uncle Ken at the wheel, the Maharaja beamed with pleasure.

'Delighted to see you, old chap!' he exclaimed. 'Jolly decent of you to drop in again. How about a game of tennis?'

Uncle Ken at the Wicket

Although restored to the Maharaja's favour, Uncle Ken was still without a job.

Granny refused to let him take the Hillman out again and

so he decided to sulk. He said it was all Grandfather's fault for not seeing to the steering wheel ten years ago, while he was still alive. Uncle Ken went on a hunger strike for two hours (between tiffin and tea), and we did not hear him whistle for several days.

'The blessedness of silence,' said Granny.

And then he announced that he was going to Lucknow to stay with Aunt Emily.

'She has three children and a school to look after,' said Granny. 'Don't stay too long.'

'She doesn't mind how long I stay,' said Uncle Ken, and off he went.

His visit to Lucknow was a memorable one, and we only heard about it much later.

When Uncle Ken got down at Lucknow station, he found himself surrounded by a large crowd, everyone waving to him and shouting words of welcome in Hindi, Urdu and English. Before he could make out what it was all about, he was smothered by garlands of marigolds. A young man came forward and announced, 'The Gomti Cricketing Association welcomes you to the historical city of Lucknow,' and promptly led Uncle Ken out of the station to a waiting car.

It was only when the car drove into the sports stadium that Uncle Ken realized that he was expected to play in a cricket match.

This is what had happened.

Bruce Hallam, the famous English cricketer, was touring India and had agreed to play in a charity match at Lucknow. But the previous evening, in Delhi, Bruce had gone to bed with an upset stomach and hadn't been able to get up in time to catch the train. A telegram was sent to the organizers of the match in Lucknow; but, like many a telegram, it did not reach its destination. The cricket fans of Lucknow had arrived at the station in droves to welcome the great cricketer. And by a strange coincidence, Uncle Ken bore a startling resemblance to Bruce Hallam; even the bald patch on the crown of his head was exactly like Hallam's. Hence the muddle. And, of course, Uncle Ken was always happy to enter into the spirit of a muddle.

Having received from the Gomti Cricketing Association a rousing reception and a magnificent breakfast at the stadium, he felt that it would be very unsporting on his part if he refused to play cricket for them. 'If I can hit a tennis ball,' he mused, 'I ought to be able to hit a cricket ball.' And luckily there was a blazer and a pair of white flannels in his suitcase.

The Gomti team won the toss and decided to bat. Uncle Ken was expected to go in at number three, Bruce Hallam's normal position. And he soon found himself walking to the wicket, wondering why on earth no one had as yet invented a more comfortable kind of pad.

The first ball he received was short-pitched, and he was able to deal with it in tennis fashion, swatting it to the midwicket boundary. He got no runs, but the crowd cheered.

The next ball took Uncle Ken on the pad. He was right in front of his wicket and should have been given out lbw. But the umpire hesitated to raise his finger. After all, hundreds of people had paid good money to see Bruce Hallam play, and it would have been a shame to disappoint them. 'Not out,' said the umpire.

The third ball took the edge of Uncle Ken's bat and sped through the slips.

'Lovely shot!' exclaimed an elderly gentleman in the pavilion.
'A classic late cut,' said another.

The ball reached the boundary and Uncle Ken had four runs to his name. Then it was 'over', and the other batsman had to face the bowling. He took a run off the first ball and called for a second run.

Uncle Ken thought one run was more than enough. Why go charging up and down the wicket like a mad man? However, he couldn't refuse to run, and he was halfway down the pitch when the fielder's throw hit the wicket. Uncle Ken was run out by yards. There could be no doubt about it this time,

He returned to the pavilion to the sympathetic applause of the crowd.

'Not his fault,' said the elderly gentleman. 'The other chap shouldn't have called. There wasn't a run there. Still, it was worth coming here all the way from Kanpur, if only to see that superb late cut...'

♦

Uncle Ken enjoyed a hearty tiffin, and then, realizing that the Gomti team would probably have to be in the field for most of the afternoon—more running about!—he slipped out of the pavilion, left the stadium, and took a tonga to Aunt Emily's house in the cantonment.

He was just in time for a second lunch (taken at one o'clock) with Aunt Emily's family: and it was presumed at the stadium that Bruce Hallam had left early to catch the train to Allahabad, where he was expected to play in another charity match.

Aunt Emily, a forceful woman, fed Uncle Ken for a week, and then put him to work in the boys' dormitory of her school. It was several months before he was able to save up enough money to run away and return to Granny's place.

But he had the satisfaction of knowing that he had helped

the great Bruce Hallam to add another four runs to his grand aggregate. The scorebook of the Gomti Cricketing Association had recorded his feat for all time:

'B. Hallam run out at 1.'

The Gomti team lost the match. But, as Uncle Ken would readily admit, where would we be without losers?

AT SEA WITH UNCLE KEN

With uncle Ken you always had to expect the unexpected. Even in the most normal circumstances, something unusual would happen to him and to those around him. He was a catalyst for confusion.

My mother should have known better than to ask him to accompany me to England the year after I'd finished school. She felt that a boy of sixteen was a little too young to make the voyage on his own; I might get lost or lose my money or fall overboard or catch some dreadful disease. She should have realized that Uncle Ken, her only brother (well spoilt by his five sisters), was more likely to do all these things.

Anyway, he was put in charge of me and instructed to deliver me safely to my aunt in England, after which he could either stay there or return to India, whichever he preferred. Granny had paid for his ticket; so in effect he was getting a free holiday which included a voyage on a posh P&O liner.

Our train journey to Bombay passed off without incident, although Uncle Ken did manage to misplace his spectacles, getting down at the station wearing someone else's. This left him a little short-sighted, which might have accounted for his mistaking the stationmaster for a porter and instructing him to look after our luggage.

We had two days in Bombay before boarding the *S.S. Strathnaver* and Uncle Ken vowed that we would enjoy ourselves. However, he was a little constrained by his budget and took me to a rather seedy hotel on Lamington Road, where we had to share a toilet with over twenty other people.

'Never mind,' he said. 'We won't spend much time in this dump.' So he took me to Marine Drive and the Gateway of India and to an Irani restaurant in Colaba, where we enjoyed a super dinner of curried prawns and scented rice. I don't know if it was the curry, the prawns or the scent, but Uncle Ken was up all night, running back and forth to that toilet, so that no one else had a chance to use it. Several dispirited travellers simply opened their windows and ejected into space, cursing Uncle Ken all the while.

He had recovered by morning and proposed a trip to the Elephanta Caves. After a breakfast of fish pickle, Malabar chilli chutney and sweet Gujarati puris, we got into a launch, accompanied by several other tourists and set off on our short cruise. The sea was rather choppy and we hadn't gone far before Uncle Ken decided to share his breakfast with the fishes of the sea. He was as green as a seaweed by the time we were ashore. Uncle Ken collapsed on the sand and refused to move, so we didn't see much of the caves. I brought him some coconut water and he revived a bit and suggested we go on a fast until it was time to board our ship.

We were safely on board the following morning, and the ship sailed majestically out from Ballard Pier, Bombay, and India receded into the distance, quite possibly forever as I wasn't sure that I would ever return. The sea fascinated me and I remained on deck all day, gazing at small crafts, passing steamers, sea birds, the distant shoreline, salt water smells, the surge of the waves and, of course, my fellow passengers. I could well understand the fascination it held for writers such as Conrad, Stevenson, Maugham and others.

Uncle Ken, however, remained confined to his cabin. The rolling of the ship made him feel extremely ill. If he had been looking green in Bombay, he was looking yellow at sea. I took my meals in the dining saloon, where I struck up an acquaintance with a well-known palmist and fortune teller who was on his way to London to make his fortune. He looked at my hand and told me I'd never be rich, but that I'd help other people get rich!

When Uncle Ken felt better (on the third day of the voyage), he struggled up on the deck, took a large lungful of sea air and subsided into a deck chair. He dozed the day away, but was suddenly wide awake when an attractive blonde strode past us on her way to the lounge. After some time we heard the tinkling of a piano. Intrigued, Uncle Ken rose and staggered into the lounge. The girl was at the piano, playing something classical which wasn't something that Uncle Ken normally enjoyed, but he was smitten by the girl's good looks and stood enraptured, his eyes brightly gleaming, his jaw sagging. With his nose pressed against the glass of the lounge door, he reminded me of a goldfish who had fallen in love with an angelfish that had just been introduced into the tank.

'What is she playing?' he whispered, aware that I had grown up on my father's classical record collection.

'Rachmaninoff,' I made a guess. 'Or maybe Rimsky–Korsakov.'

'Something easier to pronounce,' he begged.

'Chopin,' I said.

'And what's his most famous composition?'

'"Polonaise in E flat". Or maybe it's E minor.'

He pushed open the lounge door, walked in, and when the girl had finished playing, applauded loudly. She acknowledged his applause with a smile and then went on to play something else.

When she had finished he clapped again and said, 'Wonderful! Chopin never sounded better!'

'Actually, it's Tchaikovsky,' said the girl. But she didn't seem to mind.

Uncle Ken would turn up at all her practice sessions and very soon they were strolling the decks together. She was Australian, on her way to London to pursue a musical career as a concert pianist. I don't know what she saw in Uncle Ken, but he knew all the right people. And he was quite good-looking in an effete sort of way.

Left to my own devices, I followed my fortune-telling friend around and watched him study the palms of our fellow passengers. He foretold romance, travel, success, happiness, health, wealth and longevity, but never predicted anything that might upset anyone. As he did not charge anything (he was, after all, on holiday) he proved to be a popular passenger throughout the voyage. Later he was to become quite famous as a palmist and mind reader, an Indian 'Cheiro', much in demand in the capitals of Europe.

The voyage lasted eighteen days, with stops for passengers and cargo at Aden, Port Said and Marseilles, in that order. It was at Port Said that Uncle Ken and his friend went ashore, to look at the sights and do some shopping.

'You stay on the ship,' Uncle Ken told me. 'Port Said isn't safe for young boys.'

He wanted the girl all to himself, of course. He couldn't have shown off with me around. His 'man of the world' manner would not have been very convincing in my presence.

The ship was due to sail again that evening and passengers had to be back on board an hour before departure. The hours passed easily enough for me as the little library kept me engrossed.

If there are books around, I am never bored. Towards evening, I went up on deck and saw Uncle Ken's friend coming up the gangway; but of Uncle Ken there was no sign.

'Where's Uncle?' I asked her.

'Hasn't he returned? We got separated in a busy marketplace and I thought he'd get here before me.'

We stood at the railings and looked up and down the pier, expecting to see Uncle Ken among the other returning passengers. But he did not turn up.

'I suppose he's looking for you,' I said. 'He'll miss the boat if he doesn't hurry.'

The ship's hooter sounded. 'All aboard!' called the captain on his megaphone. The big ship moved slowly out of the harbour. We were on our way! In the distance I saw a figure that looked like Uncle Ken running along the pier, frantically waving his arms. But there was no turning back.

A few days later my aunt met me at Tilbury Dock.

'Where's your Uncle Ken?' she asked.

'He stayed behind at Port Said. He went ashore and didn't get back in time.'

'Just like Ken. And I don't suppose he has much money with him. Well, if he gets in touch we'll send him a postal order.'

But Uncle Ken failed to get in touch. He was a topic of discussion for several days, while I settled down in my aunt's house and looked for a job. At sixteen, I was working in an office, earning a modest salary and contributing towards my aunt's housekeeping expenses. There was no time to worry about Uncle Ken's whereabouts.

My readers know that I longed to return to India, but it was nearly four years before that became possible. Finally I did come home and as the train drew into Dehra's little station,

I looked out of the window and saw a familiar figure on the platform. It was Uncle Ken!

He made no reference to his disappearance at Port Said, and greeted me as though we had last seen each other the previous day.

'I've hired a cycle for you,' he said. 'Feel like a ride?'

'Let me get home first, Uncle Ken. I've got all this luggage.'

The luggage was piled into a tonga, I sat on top of everything and we went clip-clopping down an avenue of familiar litchi trees (all gone now, I fear). Uncle Ken rode behind the tonga, whistling cheerfully.

'When did you get back to Dehra?' I asked.

'Oh, a couple of years ago. Sorry I missed the boat. Was the girl upset?'

'She said she'd never forgive you.'

'Oh well, I expect she's better off without me. Fine piano player. Chopin and all that stuff.'

'Did Granny send you the money to come home?'

'No, I had to take a job working as a waiter in a Greek restaurant. Then I took tourists to look at the pyramids. I'm an expert on pyramids now. Great place, Egypt. But I had to leave when they found I had no papers or permit. They put me on a boat to Aden. Stayed in Aden six months teaching English to the son of a shiekh. Shiekh's son went to England, I came back to India.'

'And what are you doing now, Uncle Ken?'

'Thinking of starting a poultry farm. Lots of space behind your Gran's house. Maybe you can help with it.'

'I couldn't save much money, Uncle.'

'We'll start in a small way. There is a big demand for eggs, you know. Everyone's into eggs—scrambled, fried, poached, boiled.

Egg curry for lunch. Omelettes for dinner. Egg sandwiches for tea. How do you like your egg?'

'Fried,' I said. 'Sunny side up.'

'We shall have fried eggs for breakfast. Funny side up!'

The poultry farm never did happen, but it was good to be back in Dehra, with the prospect of limitless bicycle rides with Uncle Ken.

UNCLE KEN'S FEATHERED FOES

Uncle Ken looked smug and pleased with life. He had just taken a large bite out of a currant bun (well-buttered inside, with strawberry jam as a filling) and was about to take a second bite when, out of a clear blue sky, a hawk swooped down, snatched the bun out of Uncle Ken's hands and flew away with its trophy.

It was a bad time for Uncle Ken. He was being persecuted—not by his sisters or the world at large, but by the birds in our compound.

It all began when he fired his airgun at a noisy bunch of crows, and one of them fell dead on the veranda steps.

The crows never forgave him.

He had only to emerge from the house for a few minutes, and they would fling themselves at him, a noisy gang of ten to fifteen crows, swooping down with flapping wings and extended beaks, knocking off his hat and clawing at his flailing arms. If Uncle Ken wanted to leave the compound, he would have to sneak out of the back veranda, make a dash for his bicycle, and pedal furiously down the driveway until he was out of the gate and on the main road. Even then, he would be pursued by two or three outraged crows until he was well outside their territory.

This persecution continued for two or three weeks, until, in desperation, Uncle Ken adopted a disguise. He put on a false beard, a deerstalker cap (in the manner of Sherlock Holmes), a long black cloak (in the manner of Count Dracula), and a pair of Grandfather's old riding boots. And so attired, he marched up and down the driveway, frightening away two elderly ladies who had come to see Grandmother. The crows were suitably baffled and kept at a distance. But Granny's pet mongrel, Crazy, began barking furiously, caught hold of Uncle Ken's cloak and wouldn't let go until I came to his rescue.

◆

The mango season was approaching, and we were all looking forward to feasting on our mangoes that summer.

There were three or four mango trees in our compound, and Uncle Ken was particularly anxious to protect them from monkeys, parrots, flying foxes and other fruit-eating creatures. He had his own favourite mango tree, and every afternoon he would place a cot beneath it, and whenever he spotted winged or furred intruders in the tree, he would put a small bugle to his lips and produce a shrill bugle call—loud enough to startle everyone in the house as well as the denizens of the trees.

However, after a few shattering bugle calls Uncle Ken would doze off, only to wake up an hour later bespattered with the droppings of parrots, pigeons, squirrels, and other inhabitants of the mango tree. After two or three days of blessings from the birds, Uncle Ken came out with a large garden umbrella which protected him from aerial bombardment.

While he was fast asleep one afternoon (after spoiling Grandfather's siesta with his horn blowing), Granny caught me by the hand and said, 'Be a good boy; go out and fetch that bugle.'

I did as I was told, slipping the bugle out of Uncle Ken's hands as he snored, and handed it over to Granny. I'm not sure what she did with it, but a few weeks later, as a wedding band came down the road, drums beating and trumpets blaring, I thought I recognized Uncle Ken's old bugle. A dark, good-looking youth blew vigorously upon it, quite out of tune with everyone else. It looked and sounded like Uncle Ken's bugle.

◆

Summer came and went, and so did the mangoes. And then the monsoon arrived, and the pond behind the house overflowed, and there were frogs hopping about all over the veranda.

One morning Grandfather called me over to the back garden and led me down to the pond where he pointed to a couple of new arrivals—a pair of colourful storks who were wading about on their long legs and using their huge bills to snap up fish, frogs, or anything else they fancied. They paid no attention to us, and we were quite content to watch them going about their business.

Uncle Ken, of course, had to go and make a nuisance of himself. Armed with his Kodak 'Baby Brownie' camera (all the rage at the time), he waded into the pond (wearing Grandfather's boots) and proceeded to take pictures of the visiting birds.

Now, certain storks and cranes—especially those who move about in pairs—grow very attached to each other, and resent any overtures of friendship from clumsy humans.

Mr Stork, seeing Uncle Ken approaching through the lily-covered waters, assumed that my uncle's intentions were of an amorous nature. Uncle Ken in hat and cloak might well have been mistaken for a huge bird of prey—or a member of the ostrich family.

Mr Stork wasn't going to stand for any rivals, and leaving Mrs Stork to do the fishing, advanced upon Uncle Ken with surprising speed, lunged at him, and knocked the camera from his hands.

Leaving his camera to the tadpoles, Uncle Ken fled from the lily pond, hotly pursued by an irate stork, who even got in a couple of kung-fu kicks before Uncle Ken reached the safety of the veranda.

Mourning the loss of his dignity and his camera, Uncle Ken sulked for a couple of days, and then announced that he was going to far-off Pondicherry, to stay with an aunt who had settled there.

Everyone heaved a sigh of relief, and Grandfather and I saw Uncle Ken off at the station, just to make sure he didn't change his mind and return home in time for dinner.

Later, we heard that Uncle Ken's holiday in Pondicherry went smoothly for a couple of days, there being no trees around his aunt's seafront flat. On the beach he consumed innumerable ice creams and platters full of French fries, without being bothered by crows, parrots, monkeys or small boys.

And then, one morning, he decided to treat himself to breakfast at an open-air cafe near the beach, and ordered bacon and eggs, sausages, three toasts, cheese and marmalade.

He had barely taken a bite out of his buttered toast when, out of a blind blue sky, a seagull swooped down and carried off a sausage.

Uncle Ken was still in shock when another seagull shot past him, taking with it a rasher of bacon.

Seconds later, a third gull descended and removed the remaining sausage, splattering toast and fried egg all over Uncle Ken's trousers.

He was left with half a toast and a small pot of marmalade.

When he got back to the flat and told his aunt what had

happened, she felt sorry for him and gave him a glass of milk and a peanut-butter sandwich.

Uncle Ken hated milk. And he detested peanut butter. But when hungry, he would eat almost anything.

'Can't trust those seagulls,' said his aunt. 'They are all non-veg. Stick to spinach and lettuce, and they'll leave you alone.'

'Ugh,' said Uncle Ken in disgust. 'I'd rather be a seagull.'

ESCAPE FROM JAVA

'No one, it seemed, was interested in defending Java, only in getting out as fast as possible.'

It all happened within the space of a few days. The cassia tree had barely come into flower when the first bombs fell on Batavia (now called Jakarta) and the bright pink blossoms lay scattered over the wreckage in the streets.

News had reached us that Singapore had fallen to the Japanese. My father said: 'I expect it won't be long before they take Java. With the British defeated, how can the Dutch be expected to win?' He did not mean to be critical of the Dutch; he knew they did not have the backing of an Empire such as Britain then had. Singapore had been called the Gibraltar of the East. After its surrender there could only be retreat, a vast exodus of Europeans from Southeast Asia.

It was World War II. What the Javanese thought about the war is now hard for me to say, because I was only nine at the time and knew little of worldly matters. Most people knew they would be exchanging their Dutch-rulers for Japanese rulers; but there were also many who spoke in terms of freedom for Java when the war was over.

Our neighbor, Mr Hartono, was one of those who looked ahead to a time when Java, Sumatra, and the other islands would make up one independent nation. He was a college professor and spoke Dutch, Chinese, Javanese and a little English. His son, Sono, was about my age. He was the only boy I knew who could talk to me in English, and as a result we spent a lot of time together. Our favourite pastime was flying kites in the park.

The bombing soon put an end to kite flying. Air raid alerts sounded at all hours of the day and night, and although in the beginning most of the bombs fell near the docks, a couple of miles from where we lived, we had to stay indoors. If the planes sounded very near, we dived under beds or tables. I don't remember if there were any trenches. Probably there hadn't been time for trench digging, and now there was time only for digging graves. Events had moved all too swiftly, and everyone (except, of course, the Javanese) was anxious to get away from Java.

'When are you going?' asked Sono, as we sat on the veranda steps in a pause between air raids.

'I don't know,' I said. 'It all depends on my father.'

'My father says the Japs will be here in a week. And if you're still here then, they'll put you to work building a railway.'

'I wouldn't mind building a railway,' I said.

'But they won't give you enough to eat. Just rice with worms in it. And if you don't work properly they'll shoot you.'

'They do that to soldiers,' I said. 'We're civilians.'

'They do it to civilians, too,' said Sono.

What were my father and I doing in Batavia, when our home had been first in India and then in Singapore? He worked for a firm dealing in rubber, and six months earlier he had been sent to Batavia to open a new office in partnership with a Dutch business house. Although I was so young, I accompanied my father almost everywhere. My mother had died when I was very small, and my father had always looked after me. After the war was over, he was going to take me to England.

'Are we going to win the war?' I asked.

'It doesn't look it from here,' he said.

No, it didn't look as though we were winning. Standing at the docks with my father, I watched the ships arrive from Singapore, crowded with refugees—men, women and children all living on the decks in the hot tropical sun; they looked pale and worn out and worried. They were on their way to Colombo or Bombay. No one came ashore at Batavia. It wasn't British territory; it was Dutch, and everyone knew it wouldn't be Dutch for long.

'Aren't we going too?' I asked. 'Sono's father says the Japs will be here any day.'

'We've still got a few days,' said my father. He was a short, stocky man who seldom got excited. If he was worried, he didn't show it. 'I've got to wind up a few business matters, and then we'll be off.'

'How will we go? There's no room for us on those ships.'

'There certainly isn't. But we'll find a way, lad, don't worry.'

I didn't worry. I had complete confidence in my father's ability to find a way out of difficulties. He used to say, 'Every problem has a solution hidden away somewhere, and if only you look hard enough enough you will find it.'

There were British soldiers in the streets but they did not make us feel much safer. They were just waiting for troop ships to come and take them away. No one, it seemed, was interested in defending Java, only in getting out as fast as possible.

Although the Dutch were unpopular with the Javanese people, there was no ill-feeling against individual Europeans. I could walk safely through the streets. Occasionally, small boys in the crowded Chinese quarter would point at me and shout, *'Orang Balandi!'* (Dutchman!) but they did so in good humour, and I didn't know the language well enough to stop and explain that the English weren't Dutch. For them, all white people were the same, and understandably so.

My father's office was in the commercial area, along the canal banks. Our two-storied house, about a mile away, was an old building with a roof of red tiles and a broad balcony which had stone dragons at either end. There were flowers in the garden almost all the year round. If there was anything in Batavia more regular than the bombing, it was the rain, which came pattering down on the roof and on the banana fronds almost every afternoon. In the hot and steamy atmosphere of Java, the rain was always welcome.

There were no anti-aircraft guns in Batavia—at least we never heard any—and the Jap bombers came over at will, dropping their bombs by daylight. Sometimes bombs fell in the town. One day the building next to my father's office received a direct hit and tumbled into the river. A number of office workers were killed.

One day Sono said, 'The bombs are falling on Batavia, not in the countryside. Why don't we get cycles and ride out of town?'

I fell in with the idea at once. After the morning all-clear had sounded, we mounted our cycles and rode out of town. Mine was a hired cycle, but Sono's was his own. He'd had it since the age of five, and it was constantly in need of repairs. 'The soul has gone out of it,' he used to say.

Our fathers were at work; Sono's mother had gone out to do her shopping (during air raids she took shelter under the most convenient shop counter) and wouldn't be back for at least an hour. We expected to be back before lunch.

We were soon out of town, on a road that passed through rice fields, pineapple orchards and cinchona plantations. On our right lay dark green hills; on our left, groves of coconut palms, and beyond them, the sea. Men and women were working in the rice fields, knee-deep in mud, their broad-brimmed hats protecting them from the fierce sun. Here and there a buffalo wallowed in a pool of brown water, while a naked boy lay stretched out on the animal's broad back.

We took a bumpy track through the palms. They grew right down to the edge of the sea. Leaving our cycles on the shingle, we ran down a smooth, sandy beach and into the shallow water.

'Don't go too far in,' warned Sono. 'There may be sharks about.'

Wading in amongst the rocks, we searched for interesting shells, then sat down on a large rock and looked out to sea, where a sailing ship moved placidly on the crisp blue waters. It was difficult to imagine that half the world was at war, and that Batavia, two or three miles away, was right in the middle of it.

On our way home we decided to take a short cut through the rice fields, but soon found that our tires got bogged down in the soft mud. This delayed our return; and to make things worse, we got the roads mixed up and reached an area of the town that seemed unfamiliar. We had barely entered the outskirts when the siren sounded, to be followed soon after by the drone of approaching aircraft.

'Should we get off our cycles and take shelter somewhere?' I called out.

'No, let's race home!' shouted Sono. 'The bombs won't fall here.'

But he was wrong. The planes flew in very low. Looking up for a moment, I saw the sun blotted out by the sinister shape of a Jap fighter-bomber. We pedalled furiously, but we had barely covered fifty yards when there was a terrific explosion on our right, behind some houses. The shock sent us spinning across the road. We were flung from our cycles. And the cycles, still propelled by the blast, crashed into a wall.

I felt a stinging sensation in my hands and legs, as though scores of little insects had bitten me. Tiny droplets of blood appeared here and there on my flesh. Sono was on all fours, crawling beside me, and I saw that he too had the same small scratches on his hands and forehead, made by tiny shards of flying glass.

We were quickly on our feet, and then we began running in the general direction of our homes. The twisted cycles lay forgotten in the road.

'Get off the street, you two!' shouted someone from a window; but we weren't going to stop running until we got home. And we ran faster than we'd ever run in our lives.

My father and Sono's parents were themselves running about the street, calling for us, when we came rushing around the corner and tumbled into their arms.

'Where have you been?'

'What happened to you?'

'How did you get those cuts?'

All superfluous questions; but before we could recover our breath and start explaining, we were bundled into our respective homes. My father washed my cuts and scratches, dabbed at my face and legs with iodine—ignoring my yelps—and then stuck plaster all over my face.

Sono and I had both had a fright, and we did not venture far from the house again.

That night my father said, 'I think we'll able to leave in a day or two.'

'Has another ship come in?'

'No.'

'Then how are we going? By plane?'

'Wait and see, lad. It isn't settled yet. But we won't be able to take much with us—just enough to fill a couple of travelling bags.'

'What about the stamp collection?' I asked.

My father's stamp collection was quite valuable, and filled several volumes.

'I'm afraid we'll have to leave most of it behind,' he said. 'Perhaps Mr Hartono will keep it for me, and when the war is over—if it's ever over—we'll come back for it.'

'But we can take one or two albums with us, can't we?'

'I'll take one. There'll be room for one. Then if we're short of money in Bombay, we can sell the stamps.'

'Bombay? That's in India. I thought we were going back to England.'

'First we must go to India.'

The following morning I found Sono in the garden, patched up like me, and with one foot in a bandage. But he was as cheerful as ever and gave me his usual wide grin.

'We're leaving tomorrow,' I said.

The grin left his face.

'I will be sad when you go,' he said. 'But I will be glad, too, because then you will be able to escape from the Japs.'

'After the war, I'll come back.'

'Yes, you must come back. And then, when we are big, we will go round the world together. I want to see England and America and Africa and India and Japan. I want to go everywhere.'

'We can't go everywhere.'

'Yes, we can. No one can stop us!'

We had to be up very early the next morning. Our bags had been packed late at night. We were taking a few clothes, some of my father's business papers, a pair of binoculars, one stamp album, and several bars of chocolate. I was pleased about the stamp album and the chocolates, but I had to give up several of my treasures—favourite books, the gramophone and records, an old Samurai sword, a train set and a dartboard. The only consolation was that Sono, and not a stranger, would have them.

In the first faint light of dawn a truck drew up in front of the house. It was driven by a Dutch businessman, Mr Hookens, who worked with my father. Sono was already at the gate, waiting to say goodbye.

'I have a present for you,' he said.

He took me by the hand and pressed a smooth, hard object into my palm. I grasped it and then held it up against the light. It was a beautiful little sea horse, carved out of pale blue jade.

'It will bring you luck,' said Sono.

'Thank you,' I said. 'I will keep it forever.'

And I slipped the little sea horse into my pocket.

'In you get, lad,' said my father, and I got up on the front seat between him and Mr Hookens.

As the truck started up, I turned to wave to Sono. He was sitting on his garden wall, grinning at me. He called out, 'We will go everywhere, and no one can stop us!'

He was still waving when the truck took us round the bend at the end of the road.

We drove through the still, quiet streets of Batavia, occasionally passing burnt-out trucks and shattered buildings. Then we left the sleeping city far behind and were climbing into the forested hills. It had rained during the night, and when the sun came up over the green hills, it twinkled and glittered on the broad, wet leaves. The light in the forest changed from dark green to greenish gold, broken here and there by the flaming red or orange of a trumpet-shaped blossom. It was impossible to know the names of all those fantastic plants! The road had been cut through dense tropical forest, and on either side, the trees jostled each other, hungry for the sun; but they were chained together by the liana creepers and vines that fed upon the same struggling trees.

Occasionally a Jelarang, a large Javan squirrel, frightened by the passing of the truck, leapt through the trees before disappearing into the depths of the forest. We saw many birds: peacocks, jungle fowl, and once, standing majestically at the side of the road, a crowned pigeon, its great size and splendid crest making it a striking object even at a distance. Mr Hookens slowed down so that we could look at the bird. It bowed its head so that its crest swept the ground; then it emitted a low, hollow boom rather like the call of a turkey.

When we came to a small clearing, we stopped for breakfast. Butterflies—black, green and gold—flitted across the clearing. The silence of the forest was broken only by the drone of airplanes, Japanese Zeros heading for Batavia on another raid. I thought about Sono, and wondered what he would be doing at home: probably trying out the gramophone!

We ate boiled eggs and drank tea from a thermos, then got

back into the truck and resumed our journey.

I must have dozed off soon after because the next thing I remember is that we were going quite fast down a steep, winding road, and in the distance I could see a calm blue lagoon.

'We've reached the sea again,' I said.

'That's right,' said my father. 'But we're now nearly a hundred miles from Batavia, in another part of the island. You're looking out over the Sunda Straits.'

Then he pointed towards a shimmering white object resting on the waters of the lagoon.

'There's our plane,' he said.

'A seaplane!' I exclaimed. 'I never guessed. Where will it take us?'

'To India, I hope. There aren't many other places left to go to!'

It was a very old seaplane, and no one, not even the captain—the pilot was called the captain—could promise that it would take off. Mr Hookens wasn't coming with us; he said the plane would be back for him the next day. Besides my father and me, there were four other passengers, and all but one were Dutch. The odd man out was a Londoner, a motor mechanic who'd been left behind in Java when his unit was evacuated. (He told us later that he'd fallen asleep at a bar in the Chinese quarter, waking up some hours after his regiment had moved off!) He looked rather scruffy. He'd lost the top button of his shirt, but instead of leaving his collar open, as we did, he'd kept it together with a large safety pin, which thrust itself out from behind a bright pink tie.

'It's a relief to find you here, guvnor,' he said, shaking my father by the hand. 'Knew you for a Yorkshireman the minute I set eyes on you. It's the *song fried* that does it, if you know what I mean.' (He meant *sang froid*, French for a 'cool look'.) 'And here I was, with all these flippin' forriners, and me not knowing a word of what they've been yattering about. Do you think this old tub will get us back to Blighty?'

'It does look a bit shaky,' said my father. 'One of the first flying boats, from the looks of it. If it gets us to Bombay, that's far enough.'

'Anywhere out of Java's good enough for me,' said our new companion. 'The name's Muggeridge.'

'Pleased to know you, Mr Muggeridge,' said my father. 'I'm Bond. This is my son.'

Mr Muggeridge rumpled my hair and favoured me with a large wink.

The captain of the seaplane was beckoning to us to join him in a small skiff which was about to take us across a short stretch of water to the seaplane.

'Here we go,' said Mr Muggeridge. 'Say your prayers and keep your fingers crossed.'

The seaplane was a long time getting airborne. It had to make several runs before it finally took off; then, lurching drunkenly, it rose into the clear blue sky.

'For a moment I thought we were going to end up in the briny,' said Mr Muggeridge, untying his seat belt. 'And talkin' of fish, I'd give a week's wages for a plate of fish an' chips and a pint of beer.'

'I'll buy you a beer in Calcutta,' said my father.

'Have an egg,' I said, remembering we still had some boiled eggs in one of the travelling bags.

'Thanks, mate,' said Mr Muggeridge, accepting an egg with alacrity. 'A real egg, too! I've been livin' on egg powder these last six months. That's what they give you in the army. And it ain't hens' eggs they make it from, let me tell you. It's either gulls' or turtles' eggs!'

'No,' said my father with a straight face. 'Snakes' eggs.'

Mr Muggeridge turned a delicate shade of green; but he soon recovered his poise, and for about an hour kept talking about almost everything under the sun, including Churchill, Hitler, Roosevelt, Mahatma Gandhi and Betty Grable. (The last-named was famous for her beautiful legs.) He would have gone on talking all the way to India had he been given a chance, but suddenly a shudder passed through the old plane, and it began lurching again.

'I think an engine is giving trouble,' said my father.

When I looked through the small glassed-in window, it seemed as though the sea was rushing up to meet us.

The co-pilot entered the passenger cabin and said something in Dutch. The passengers looked dismayed, and immediately began fastening their seat belts.

'Well, what did the blighter say?' asked Mr Muggeridge.

'I think he's going to have to ditch the plane,' said my father, who knew enough Dutch to get the gist of anything that was said.

'Down in the drink!' exclaimed Mr Muggeridge. 'Gawd 'elp us! And how far are we from India, guv?'

'A few hundred miles,' said my father.

'Can you swim, mate?' asked Mr Muggeridge looking at me.

'Yes,' I said. 'But not all the way to Bombay. How far can you swim?'

'The length of a bathtub,' he said.

'Don't worry,' said my father. 'Just make sure your life jacket's properly tied.'

We looked to our life jackets; my father checked mine twice, making sure that it was properly fastened.

The pilot had now cut both engines, and was bringing the plane down in a circling movement. But he couldn't control the speed, and it was tilting heavily to one side. Instead of landing smoothly on its belly, it came down on a wing tip, and this caused the plane to swivel violently around in the choppy sea. There was a terrific jolt when the plane hit the water, and if it hadn't been for the seat belts, we'd have been flung from our seats. Even so, Mr Muggeridge struck his head against the seat in front, and he was now holding a bleeding nose and using some shocking language.

As soon as the plane came to a standstill, my father undid my seat belt. There was no time to lose. Water was already filling the cabin, and all the passengers—except one, who was dead in his seat with a broken neck—were scrambling for the exit hatch. The co-pilot pulled a lever and the door fell away to reveal high waves slapping against the sides of the stricken plane.

Holding me by the hand, my father was leading me towards the exit.

'Quick, lad,' he said. 'We won't stay afloat for long.'

'Give us a hand!' shouted Mr Muggeridge, still struggling with his life jacket. 'First this bloody bleedin' nose, and now something's gone and stuck.'

My father helped him fix the life jacket, then pushed him out of the door ahead of us.

As we swam away from the seaplane (Mr Muggeridge splashing furiously alongside us), we were aware of the other passengers in the water. One of them shouted to us in Dutch to follow him.

We swam after him towards the dinghy, which had been

released the moment we hit the water. That yellow dinghy, bobbing about on the waves, was as welcome as land.

All who had left the plane managed to climb into the dinghy. We were seven altogether—a tight fit. We had hardly settled down in the well of the dinghy when Mr Muggeridge, still holding his nose, exclaimed, 'There she goes!' And as we looked on helplessly, the seaplane sank swiftly and silently beneath the waves.

The dinghy had shipped a lot of water, and soon everyone was busy bailing it out with mugs (there were a couple in the dinghy), hats and bare hands. There was a light swell, and every now and then water would roll in again and half fill the dinghy. But within half an hour, we had most of the water out, and then it was possible to take turns, two men doing the bailing while the others rested. No one expected me to do this work, but I took a hand anyway, using my father's sola-topee for the purpose.

'Where are we?' asked one of the passengers.

'A long way from anywhere,' said another.

'There must be a few islands in the Indian Ocean.'

'But we may be at sea for days before we come to one of them.'

'Days or even weeks,' said the captain. 'Let us look at our supplies.'

The dinghy appeared to be fairly well-provided with emergency rations: biscuits, raisins, chocolates (we'd lost our own), and enough water to last a week. There was also a first-aid box, which was put to immediate use, as Mr Muggeridge's nose needed attention. A few others had cuts and bruises. One of the passengers had received a hard knock on the head and appeared to be suffering from loss of memory. He had no idea how we happened to be drifting about in the middle of the

Indian Ocean; he was convinced that we were on a pleasure cruise a few miles off Batavia.

The unfamiliar motion of the dinghy, as it rose and fell in the troughs between the waves, resulted in almost everyone getting seasick. As no one could eat anything, a day's rations were saved.

The sun was very hot, but my father covered my head with a large spotted handkerchief. He'd always had a fancy for bandana handkerchiefs with yellow spots, and seldom carried fewer than two on his person; so he had one for himself too. The sola topee, well soaked in seawater, was being used by Mr Muggeridge.

It was only when I had recovered to some extent from my seasickness that I remembered the valuable stamp album, and sat up, exclaiming, 'The stamps! Did you bring the stamp album, Dad?'

He shook his head ruefully. 'It must be at the bottom of the sea by now,' he said. 'But don't worry, I kept a few rare stamps in my wallet.' And looking pleased with himself, he tapped the pocket of his bush shirt.

The dinghy drifted all day, with no one having the least idea where it might be taking us.

'Probably going round in circles,' said Mr Muggeridge pessimistically.

There was no compass and no sail, and paddling wouldn't have got us far even if we'd had paddles; we could only resign ourselves to the whims of the current and hope it would take us towards land or at least to within hailing distance of some passing ship.

The sun went down like an overripe tomato dissolving slowly in the sea. The darkness pressed down on us. It was a moonless night, and all we could see was the white foam on the crests of the waves. I lay with my head on my father's shoulder, and looked up at the stars which glittered in the remote heavens.

'Perhaps your friend Sono will look up at the sky tonight and see those same stars,' said my father. 'The world isn't so big after all.'

'All the same, there's a lot of sea around us,' said Mr Muggeridge from out of the darkness.

Remembering Sono, I put my hand in my pocket and was reassured to feel the smooth outline of the jade seahorse.

'I've still got Sono's seahorse,' I said, showing it to my father.

'Keep it carefully,' he said. 'It may bring us luck.'

'Are seahorses lucky?'

'Who knows? But he gave it to you with love, and love is like a prayer. So keep it carefully.'

I didn't sleep much that night. I don't think anyone slept. No one spoke much either, except of course Mr Muggeridge, who kept muttering something about cold beer and salami.

I didn't feel so sick the next day. By ten o'clock I was quite hungry; but breakfast consisted of two biscuits, a piece of chocolate, and a little drinking water. It was another hot day, and we were soon very thirsty, but everyone agreed that we should ration ourselves strictly.

Two or three still felt ill, but the others, including Mr Muggeridge, had recovered their appetites and normal spirits, and there was some discussion about the prospects of being picked up.

'Are there any distress-rockets in the dinghy?' asked my father. 'If we see a ship or a plane, we can fire a rocket and hope to be spotted. Otherwise there's not much chance of our being seen from a distance.'

A thorough search was made in the dinghy, but there were no rockets.

'Someone must have used them last Guy Fawkes Day,' commented Mr Muggeridge.

'They don't celebrate Guy Fawkes Day in Holland,' said my father. 'Guy Fawkes was an Englishman.'

'Ah,' said Mr Muggeridge, not in the least put out. 'I've always said, most great men are Englishmen. And what did this chap Guy Fawkes do?'

'Tried to blow up Parliament,' said my father.

That afternoon we saw our first sharks. They were enormous creatures, and as they glided backward and forward under the boat it seemed they might hit and capsize us. They went away for some time, but returned in the evening.

At night, as I lay half asleep beside my father, I felt a few drops of water strike my face. At first I thought it was the seaspray; but when the sprinkling continued, I realized that it was raining lightly.

'Rain!' I shouted, sitting up. 'It's raining!'

Everyone woke up and did their best to collect water in mugs, hats or other containers. Mr Muggeridge lay back with his mouth open, drinking the rain as it fell.

'This is more like it,' he said. 'You can have all the sun an' sand in the world. Give me a rainy day in England!'

But by early morning the clouds had passed, and the day turned out to be even hotter than the previous one. Soon we were all red and raw from sunburn. By midday even Mr Muggeridge was silent. No one had the energy to talk.

Then my father whispered, 'Can you hear a plane, lad?'

I listened carefully, and above the hiss of the waves I heard what sounded like the distant drone of a plane; but it must have been very far away, because we could not see it. Perhaps it was flying into the sun, and the glare was too much for our sore eyes; or perhaps we'd just imagined the sound.

Then the Dutchman who'd lost his memory thought he saw land, and kept pointing towards the horizon and saying, 'That's Batavia, I told you we were close to shore!' No one else saw anything. So my father and I weren't the only ones imagining things.

Said my father, 'It only goes to show that a man can see what he wants to see, even if there's nothing to be seen!'

The sharks were still with us. Mr Muggeridge began to resent them. He took off one of his shoes and hurled it at the nearest shark; but the big fish ignored the shoe and swam on after us.

'Now, if your leg had been in that shoe, Mr Muggeridge, the shark might have accepted it,' observed my father.

'Don't throw your shoes away,' said the captain. 'We might land on a deserted coastline and have to walk hundreds of miles!'

A light breeze sprang up that evening, and the dinghy moved more swiftly on the choppy water.

'At last we're moving forward,' said the captain.

'In circles,' said Mr Muggeridge.

But the breeze was refreshing; it cooled our burning limbs and helped us to get some sleep. In the middle of the night, I woke up feeling very hungry.

'Are you all right?' asked my father, who had been awake all the time.

'Just hungry,' I said.

'And what would you like to eat?'

'Oranges!'

He laughed. 'No oranges on board. But I kept a piece of my chocolate for you. And there's a little water, if you're thirsty.'

I kept the chocolate in my mouth for a long time, trying to make it last. Then I sipped a little water.

'Aren't you hungry?' I asked.

'Ravenous! I could eat a whole turkey. When we get to Calcutta or Madras or Colombo, or wherever it is we get to, we'll go to the best restaurant in town and eat like—like—'

'Like shipwrecked sailors!' I said.

'Exactly.'

'Do you think we'll ever get to land, Dad?'

'I'm sure we will. You're not afraid, are you?'

'No. Not as long as you're with me.'

Next morning, to everyone's delight, we saw seagulls. This was a sure sign that land couldn't be far away; but a dinghy could take days to drift a distance of thirty or forty miles. The birds wheeled noisily above the dinghy. Their cries were the first familiar sounds we had heard for three days and three nights, apart from the wind and the sea and our own weary voices.

The sharks had disappeared, and that too was an encouraging sign. They didn't like the oil slicks that were appearing in the water.

But presently the gulls left us, and we feared we were drifting away from land.

'Circles,' repeated Mr Muggeridge. 'Circles.'

We had sufficient food and water for another week at sea; but no one even wanted to think about spending another week at sea.

The sun was a ball of fire. Our water ration wasn't sufficient to quench our thirst. By noon, we were without much hope or energy.

My father had his pipe in his mouth. He didn't have any tobacco, but he liked holding the pipe between his teeth. He said it prevented his mouth from getting too dry.

The sharks came back.

Mr Muggeridge removed his other shoe and threw it at them.

'Nothing like a lovely wet English summer,' he mumbled.

I fell asleep in the well of the dinghy, my father's large handkerchief spread over my face. The yellow spots on the cloth seemed to grow into enormous revolving suns.

When I woke up, I found a huge shadow hanging over us. At first I thought it was a cloud. But it was a shifting shadow. My father took the handkerchief from my face and said, 'You can wake up now, lad. We'll be home and dry soon.'

A fishing boat was beside us, and the shadow came from its wide flapping sail. A number of bronzed, smiling, chattering fishermen—Burmese, as we discovered later—were gazing down at us from the deck of their boat.

A few days later, my father and I were in Calcutta.

My father sold his rare stamps for over a thousand rupees, and we were able to live in a comfortable hotel. Mr Muggeridge was flown back to England. Later we got a postcard from him saying the English rain was awful!

'And what about us?' I asked. 'Aren't we going back to England?'

'Not yet,' said my father. 'You'll be going to a boarding school in Shimla until the war's over.'

'But why should I leave you?' I asked.

'Because I've joined the RAF,' he said. 'Don't worry, I'm being posted in Delhi. I'll be able to come up to see you sometimes.'

A week later I was on a small train which went chugging up the steep mountain track to Shimla. Several Indian, Anglo-Indian and English children tumbled around in the compartment. I felt quite out of place among them, as though I had grown out of their pranks. But I wasn't unhappy. I knew my father would be coming to see me soon. He'd promised me some books, a pair of rollerskates and a cricket bat, just as soon as he got his first month's pay.

Meanwhile, I had the jade seahorse which Sono had given me.

And I have it with me today.

A WEEK IN THE JUNGLE

Grandfather never hunted wild animals, he couldn't understand the pleasure some people obtained from killing the creatures of our forests. Birds and animals, he felt, had as much right to live as humans. We could kill them for food, he said, because even animals killed for food; but not for pleasure.

At the age of twelve I did not have the same high principles as Grandfather. Nevertheless, I disliked shooting. I found it boring.

Uncle Henry and some of his sporting friends once took me on a shikar expedition into the Terai jungles in the Shivalik range. The prospect of a week in the jungle, as camp-follower to several adults with guns, filled me with dismay. I knew that long, weary hours would be spent tramping behind these tall, professional-looking huntsmen who spoke in terms of bagging this tiger or that wild elephant, when all they ever got, if they were lucky, was a wild hare or a partridge. Tigers and excitement, it seemed, came only to Jim Corbett.

This particular expedition proved to be no different from others. There were four men with guns and at the end of the week all that they had shot were two miserable, underweight wildfowl. But I managed, on our second day in the jungle, to be left behind in the rest house. And, in the course of a morning's exploration of the old bungalow, I discovered a shelf of books half-hidden in a corner of the back veranda.

Who had left them there? A literary forest officer? A

memsahib who had been bored by her husband's campfire boasting? Or someone who had no interest in the 'manly' sport of slaughtering wild animals and had brought his library along to pass the time? He must have left it behind for others like him.

Or possibly the poor fellow had gone into the jungle one day, as a gesture to his more bloodthirsty companions, and been trampled by an elephant, or gored by a wild boar, or (more likely) accidentally shot by one of the shikaris—and his sorrowing friends had taken his remains away and left his books behind.

Anyway, there it was—a shelf of some thirty volumes, in different shapes, sizes, and colours. I wiped the thick dust off the covers and examined the titles. As my reading tastes had not yet formed, I was willing to try anything. The bookshelf was varied in its contents, and my own interests have since remained fairly universal.

On that second day in the forest rest house, I discovered P.G. Wodehouse and read his *Love Among the Chickens*, an early Ukridge story and still one of my favourites. By the time the perspiring hunters came home in the evening, with their spent cartridges and impressive excuses, I had made a start with M.R. James's *Ghost Stories of an Antiquary*. This kept me awake most of the night, until the oil in the kerosene lamp was exhausted.

Next morning, fresh and optimistic again, the shikaris set out for a different area, where they hoped to get a tiger. They had employed a party of villagers to beat the jungle, and all day I could hear the tom-toms throbbing in the distance. This did not prevent me from finishing M.R. James, or discovering a little book called *A Naturalist on the Prowl* by E.H. Aitken, It described the tremendous fun and interest to be had from studying the wildlife in one's own back garden—the grasshoppers, beetles, ants, butterflies and praying mantises, all living such fascinating lives just outside (and sometimes inside) our bedroom windows.

Before I had finished the book, I was looking for spiders in the corners of the old bungalow and stalking grasshoppers in the long grass of the compound. My concentration was disturbed only once, when I looked up and saw a spotted deer crossing the open space in front of the house. The deer disappeared among the sal trees and I returned to the veranda and my book.

Dusk had fallen when I heard the party returning from the hunt. The hunters were talking loudly and seemed excited. Perhaps they had got their tiger. I put down my book and came out of the house to meet them.

'Did you get the tiger?' I asked excitedly.

'No, laddie,' said Uncle Henry. 'I think we'll get it tomorrow. You should have been with us—we saw a spotted deer!'

There were three days left and I knew I would never get through the entire bookshelf. This I did not intend doing, as not all the authors on the shelf appealed to me. I chose at random *The Wind in the Willows*, *The Jungle Book*, and *David Copperfield*.

On the day I made the literary acquaintance of Mowgli, the wolf-boy, the shikaris shot the two wildfowl already mentioned. As the party had from the first intended living off the jungle, only some tinned foods had been brought along; but two lean birds were insufficient for a party of five, and once again the meal consisted mostly of corned meat and mustard.

Next day, while the grown-ups were looking for their tiger and I was learning wisdom from the Water Rat, Toad, and other river people of *The Wind in the Willows*, an event took place which disturbed my reading for a little while.

I had noticed, on the previous day, that a number of stray mongrels—belonging to watchmen, villagers and forest-guards—

always hung about the house, waiting for scraps of food to be thrown away. It was ten o'clock in the morning (a time when wild animals seldom come into the open), when I heard a sudden yelp in the clearing. Looking up, I saw a full-grown panther making off into the jungle with one of the dogs held in its mouth. The panther had either been driven towards the house by the beaters, or had watched the party leave the bungalow and decided to help itself to a meal.

There was no one else about at the time. Since the dog was obviously dead within seconds of being seized, and the panther had disappeared, I saw no point in raising an alarm but returned to my book.

It was getting late when the shikaris returned. They were dirty, sweaty and, as usual, disappointed. This time their excuses held a note of defiance. They took their corned meat in silence. Next day, we were to return to 'civilization', and none of the hunters had anything to show for a week in the jungles of India.

'No game left in these jungles,' said the leading member of the party, famed for once having shot two man-eating tigers and a basking crocodile in rapid succession.

'It's the weather,' said another. 'No rain at all this winter.'

'Don't know what the country's coming to,' grumbled the third.

'I saw a panther this morning,' I said modestly.

In fact, I was altogether too modest. I might just as well have said, 'I saw a donkey this morning,' for all the impression I made.

'Did you really?' said the leading hunter. He glanced at the book lying beside me. 'Young Master Copperfield says he saw a panther!'

The others were only faintly amused. They did not have the energy to laugh.

'Too imaginative for his age,' said one of them. 'Comes from reading so much, I suppose.'

'If you were to get out of the house and into the jungle a little,' said Uncle Henry reproachfully, 'you might really see a panther.'

'Don't know what young fellows are coming to these days...'

'Why didn't you grab it, man, and take it to Grandfather?' And everyone laughed.

I went to bed early and left them to their tales of the 'good old days' when rhinos, cheetahs, and possibly even the legendary phoenix were still available for slaughter.

I came home with a poor reputation. My uncle's friends thought I was both a sissy and a liar. And Uncle Henry, poor man, seemed to think I was responsible for the failure of the entire expedition. He did not take me with him again. But Grandfather, when I told him all about the hunt, doubled up with laughter and said he wished he had been with us, if only to see the faces of Uncle Henry and his friends. As a measure of his delight, he bought me a copy of *David Copperfield*, for I had not been able to finish the one in the forest rest house. I finally got through it in the banyan tree, in the company of several squirrels and a very noisy cicada.